SWORDS OF FIRE
BOOK SIX OF THE SHAMAN'S TALES

Copyright
All Rights Reserved. ⌐   ⌐rt J. Ryan to be
identified as the author ⌐   ⌐rk has been asserted.
All of the characters in th⌐ ⌐ook are fictitious and any
resemblance to actual persons, living or dead, is coincidental.

Cover design by www.damonza.com

ISBN: 9798850134730
(print edition)

Trotting Fox Press

Contents

1. Forbidden Magic

Kubodin watched the enemy with a dark heart. He knew they were preparing for an attack, and it would be the worst yet. Steel had failed. Sorcery alone remained.

Dawn arced over the land in slow glory. The stars dimmed and died. The sun blossomed. Shadows fled, and by the growing light the massive host that besieged Chatchek Fortress came into clear view, by terrible increments.

The top of the right gate tower was Kubodin's accustomed spot. He came there every morning before light. In the dark, it was possible to pretend the enemy did not exist. When the sun exposed their presence though, he studied them for signs of weakness that he could use.

At a soft step behind him, loud in the dawn quiet, he turned. Ravengrim had come up the stairs.

The old shaman stepped firmly forward, but his head was down and he did not meet Kubodin's gaze. He had bad news to deliver, but it was nothing that Kubodin had not anticipated.

Kubodin studied him. The old man, ancient as he seemed, still had an air of power about him. The straggly white beard, and that he leaned on a staff, meant nothing. The body and mind might be old, but there was a spirit inside him that knew how to fight, and still had the strength of magic to do so.

"Good morning, Lord Kubodin," the shaman said.

It was not a title that Kubodin was due. It was a title from long-ago stories, for there were no lords now. Even so, it was the way of these strange shamans to speak differently. And why not? The age that was legend and story to Kubodin was the age of their birth.

"What news?" Kubodin asked. "For surely by your doleful look there is some."

The old man leaned on the staff and gazed out over the battlement at the enemy.

"They will come against us soon."

"You do not mean by sword, this time."

"No. As Shar feared. As you feared. As the Nahat feared, it will be by magic. The numbers of their shamans have increased. We sense their magic. We sense their anticipation. They will send sorcery against us. Soon."

"How soon?"

"It will not be long. More shamans arrived last night. They try to conceal themselves from us, be we know they are there. Twenty-six in total."

Kubodin noticed the old man said the last with a different tone.

"Is there some significance to that number?"

"Indeed. It is two times thirteen. It is a number of power among shamans, reserved for spells of the greatest order."

There was something the old man was holding back, but Kubodin did not need to know the import of the specific details.

"Is it worth pointing out that the Nahat are almost double the enemy's number?"

The old man still did not look at him, but rather his gaze was fixed on the army below as though he saw through the masses of soldiers and studied the shamans at the rear.

"The Nahat are a match for them, and more. Shaman to shaman, we outpower them. Even so, they plan *something*. That we know and feel. We even sense confidence from them." For the first time, Ravengrim took his gaze away from the enemy and his wise, old eyes fixed on Kubodin. "They plan a magic that does not rely on numbers. They plan something … else."

Kubodin did not quite follow the gist of that. Surely it was all about numbers, but then he reconsidered. Even with armies of men and swords, it was not just a matter of a superior force. Smaller armies could, and did, beat larger ones. Shar had proved that recently. It might be even more the case with sorcery. The plan, the leader, and the courage of those who undertook deeds mattered more.

"What do you think they'll do?"

Ravengrim looked out over the battlement again, and did not answer for some while.

"I wish I knew," he said eventually.

It was not an answer that inspired confidence. At the same time, Kubodin appreciated it. It was the truth, and he would rather work with that than guesses, which turned out to be wrong.

The shaman left him then, but gave a final warning as he did.

"Be ready, Lord Kubodin. For anything. What it will be, I do not know. But it will be bad."

He was almost gone, but Kubodin called him back.

"Yes, Lord Kubodin?"

"Maybe we don't need to know what they plan."

"My lord?"

"Let me be direct. Can you kill them before they have the chance to do whatever it is they plan."

Ravengrim did not seem surprised. "We have thought on that. We will not use magic against the enemy soldiers, but the shamans are another matter. We would kill them if we could. They are too far away though, and too wary of us. They have wards set. They keep watch. They keep us at bay, at least for the moment."

It was not what Kubodin wanted to hear, but that was not the fault of Ravengrim.

"It is what it is," he said. "If the situation changes, do it. Otherwise you, and those who defend with steel blades, will all just have to do the best we can."

It was not long after that the first signs of the impending attack came. The Nagrak horde began to chant, and a hundred drums beat out a dolorous tone. The day was clear, yet somehow the air seemed darker than it should be. Nor did the direct light of the sun give warmth.

All along the battlements the men stood silent and grim. They would fight if they could, for they had proved themselves of great courage. They could not combat sorcery though.

Kubodin pulled his axe out of the belt loop through which the handle was secured. It felt heavy in his hand, and there was something strange about it. The twin blades glittered coldly in the light. Discord it had been called since days of old, and the left blade Chaos and the right blade Spite.

The names had been chosen well, and he felt the malice inside the weapon now, alive and thirsting for blood. He held it close to him, cradling it in his arms and looked out at the enemy again.

The Nagraks ceased chanting. A hush fell over the land, but into this the drums beat slowly. Like a heartbeat they were, and there was something disconcerting in the sound.

Kubodin looked over the ramparts. To the left and right, all was the same. The defenders stood motionless, waiting for what would be thrown at them. No one doubted now that it was coming. All that remained was what form this sorcerous attack would take.

The Nahat were on the ramparts too, every one of them. Ravengrim had returned to stand by his side, evidently sensing the attack was coming even sooner than he expected.

Kubodin felt a sense of pride. This was Shar's army, and they had never known defeat. Nor would they now, whatever came at them.

Brave thoughts, he knew. Yet unfounded in truth. There were some battles that could not be won.

The magic came to a crescendo. Even the drums ceased now, and the silence of the tomb enveloped both armies despite their numbers. Like the quiet of dawn before the rush of sunrise it seemed, and then there was light.

Yet it was not light such as Kubodin had ever seen. Thirteen beams lurched up from the ground before the fortress like dead men escaping the grave, and he could give colors to them all. Even so, it seemed the beams were slicked with oil that tainted them, and their colors shifted deceptively.

The beams rose upward, towering to the same height as the rampart.

All over the land the silence was deep as the ocean, and every human eye, or eye of beast on the earth or bird of the air, was drawn to the unnatural sight.

The enemy on the field below shrank away from the strange lights. Upon the battlements, men drew their swords, or hefted spear and axe. Some with bows tried a few arrows, but those shafts winged into the light and arced down to the ground after as wisps of fire and ash.

"It cannot be," whispered Ravengrim, and the shaman stepped to the very edge of the rampart and gripped the stone battlement until his fingers were white.

"What is it?" Kubodin said. He asked what he knew every defender wanted to know – the nature of the battle they now must fight. For whatever those lights were, they were hostile. Menace radiated from them like heat from a fire.

"It is forbidden!"

"Ravengrim! Tell me. Tell me now!"

The shaman turned to him, his eyes wide and his face pale.

"Some magics are forbidden. Some sorceries are so dark that they risk not just the lives of the shamans who invoke them, but the land itself. See!" Even as he spoke, the shaman thrust out a boney arm. "The lights transform into what has truly been summoned!"

Kubodin looked back at the giant lights, and he saw what Ravengrim meant. In those flickering pillars of flame images began to form, dark and terrible.

The word caught in his throat, and his mouth suddenly dry, but he forced it out.

"Demons," he croaked.

"Demons," Ravengrim confirmed, and that word was muttered all along the battlements, and the men turned pale in fear.

The demons rose, the swirling flame enveloping them and fleshing out their forms. One was man-shaped, yet great horns curved back over his skull and his eyes sparked like red embers. Another, with a fiery whip shimmering in a taloned hand, swept his gaze over the fortress and a shadow followed it like a cloud blotting out the sun. A third, female, terrible in her beauty with flashing eyes and a cruel smile, laughed. And the sound was as thunder in the mountains that spawned a landslide of crashing rock and screeching ice.

Kubodin felt his heart hammer as though it pushed ice through his arteries. Yet in his hands was a sudden warmth, and the power inside his axe stirred.

Kubodin! Warrior of the old blood! Hear me and harken to my voice!

He went to drop the axe, but found that he merely gripped it harder. The demon inside was speaking to him, and yet no one else seemed to hear. Was this madness creeping over him?

Listen, brave warrior. Your mind is strong and true. Fear not. Fear nothing! Not even these brothers and sisters of mine that shamans have dared to summon. I can protect you.

The voice was compelling. It spoke with authority, and there was the ring of truth in its words. Who but a demon could protect against other demons?

They that come against the fortress bear you no ill will, old warrior. Rather, they could be your friend. Join with me. Join with them. Together we can be a force in the world that even shamans would fear. They would scatter before you as dry leaves before the sudden tempest! What need of Shar Fei when you can rule the world yourself?

It was true. Kubodin felt it in his bones. With allies such as these the shamans were as nothing. He could end this war. He could save Shar, for surely she was in peril and would remain so until the shamans were overthrown. Moreover, he could save the entire land, and the empire of old would be reestablished, only greater than it had been. It would endure, and nothing would topple it.

The axe was suddenly light in his hand. Or else he had grown stronger. He felt power flow through him. He felt strength and confidence. He gazed at the demons taking shape, and he did not fear them.

All around him the defenders shrank back. Some even fled the walls, and he had pity on them. Warriors could not fight demons. It was a challenge beyond their power. But him? Was there anything he could not do?

The thirteen demons took their final form, and the flames around them flickered and died out. In the flesh, they strode forward as one, and the earth trembled at their footfalls as though mountains toppled to the ground.

9

The moment of destiny had come. The future of the empire that might be hung in the balance, and the twin-bladed axe in Kubodin's hand flashed with wicked light.

2. The Pit Opens

On came the demons, and the shadow of death came with them. Yet those who remained on the ramparts, more than two thirds of the defenders, hefted high their weapons. They had tasted freedom, and they would die to keep it.

Ravengrim lifted his staff. All along the battlements the Fifty had gathered, and they did the same. Kubodin, his heart raging with emotions, stepped forward and shouted.

"Begone, demons! This is not your world. From here you have been cast out in ages past, and to the pit you shall fall again!"

The gazes of the demons turned on him, all thirteen at once. He felt the force of their glance as a blow, and he stepped back under the weight of malice directed at him. Yet he straightened, and moved forward again.

"Begone!" he cried once more. And all over the battements the command was taken up, and the defenders threw the word as a weapon at their mighty foe.

It gave the demons pause. The resistance against them was great, and demons though they were, they still faced an army. They could be killed. The old legends attested to that, and though a score of warriors, or many scores might die in the injuring of just one, an army with the will to fight them was a danger.

Kubodin knew that was the key. The stories he had heard as a child all had at the center of them the concept that the greatest weapon of the demons was fear. It was their strongest tool, for the foe who was too scared to fight was defeated before the battle could begin.

He knew that, and he knew he must give the defenders heart. The chant of *begone* rose to a high pitch, and he leaped to the top of a crenelation, raising high his axe. Even as he did so, the wicked light in the metal flared into fire that spurted skyward.

"Ye demons that come against us! Come forward and die! We will not surrender though all the pit of hell is loosed upon us! We defy you! Come! Come and taste death!"

The demons laughed, and it seemed a storm of howling winds filled the very air. It did not matter. Kubodin's words were for the defenders rather than them. Yet as he spoke the fire in the twin blades of his axe flared and leaped.

Fool! Fight them not. Make allies of them!

Again Kubodin felt the pull of the axe. There was much to be said for the idea. At the same time, there was something wrong, and his memory threw up some word of advice from his father, and the line of his forefathers back until the time of Chen Fei when the axe was first given to the family. *Trust the steel of the axe; heed nothing the magic says.*

They were wise words, but faced with destruction by an enemy that outpowered the defenders by so much, would it not be wiser to compromise?

Kubodin had forgotten the Fifty, but now Ravengrim brought them into the fray. From his staff a light flared, and likewise from all his brethren along the battlement, and the lights twined and formed a shield. It was just in time, for one of the demons raised his hand and pointed, and a bolt of lightning speared through the air at the walls.

The two magics met in thunder and shattered light. It was too bright to look at, and Kubodin held a hand over his eyes and protected his gaze. The demon fire slid off the shield like a roof shedding water. Yet the dome of light quavered and buckled. He did not think it could sustain another blow, and even as he took his hand away from his eyes it flickered out.

The Nahat were not done. They switched from defense to offense, and the shield vanished. In unison they thrust their staffs forward, and Kubodin realized they somehow communicated with one another silently.

A great wind began to blow. Nothing was felt on the battlements, yet the tempest tore at the demons and the lingering tendrils of flame that yet clothed them burst into trailing streamers of fire. It seemed to do the demons no harm, and yet Kubodin saw that the flesh of their bodies began to lose form.

The female demon, eyes flashing and long hair trailing behind her as ragged fire, thrust both her hands forward. There was a clap of thunder, and the wind subsided.

Rocked by some unseen power, the defenders stumbled backward, and then the she-demon stood proud, head high and chest out while she wove some spell. Her fingers twined like serpents, and icicles hung from them.

A cold blast of air began, and it grew in intensity. Soon sleet drove toward the rampart with it, and the sleet turned to hail. Like stones it pelted the defenders, and those with shields held them aloft. Most knelt and protected their heads with their arms.

The size of the hailstones grew, and the other demons lent their power to the she-demon. Already some men were bleeding from gashes to their heads, and some few had been knocked out. If this went on, or worsened, the defenders would flee or begin to die.

Kubodin turned to Ravengrim. "What can you do?"

"Watch!" Ravengrim answered calmly. "We are not beaten just yet."

Even as he spoke the Nahat started to chant in some strange tongue. The she-demon heard it and hissed. What language it was, Kubodin was not sure. It had the ring of Elvish to it though, which he had heard in times past.

The Nahat gathered their power, and the sleet and hail that littered the battlements hovered into the air, and then shot like an arrow at the demons.

With a howl, the she-demon turned to the side and raised both arms to protect herself. The demon with the fiery whip took a pace before the others, and he cracked the black cord so that it sparked as jagged lightning, tearing the sky. A vertical split, like the eye of a cat, cracked open and Kubodin glimpsed a desolate world, something or somewhere that was not in Alithoras, and through the gap the demon drew all the sleet and hail. With another crack of his dark whip, long as the battlements were high, the portal winked shut with fire and leaping shadows.

Kubodin was not sure what to do. One of his aides nearby had gone to his knees and sunk his head into his hands. There he rocked back and forth. All along the battlements brave men began to be overpowered by fear or despair. This was an attack beyond them.

He wished Shar were here, and he knew now how hollow were the words of the demon in the axe. He could not replace her. Shar would have a plan for this – and he had nothing. At the end, where things counted most, he had failed her. And his people.

Despair crashed over him. With it came fear, and he felt his knees buckle. All was over. Hopes, dreams and life itself. What could he do against an enemy such as this? How could he give his men heart?

He could not. He would die now, as a failure. Shar would hear of it, and she would curse his name.

But that was not true. She was not like that, and she would understand. He wanted to reject that idea, and he did not know why. Then he understood.

Magic was at play. One of the demons, or all of them, was somehow manipulating his mind. His, and all the defenders. He realized that so far, they had not attacked in any real physical sense. Not by coming against the fortress themselves. Their attacks had all been, ultimately, intended to cause despair.

And it was working. Soon, the defenders would fall. The demons need not act themselves – the army of Nagraks would be sent by the shamans to sweep over the fortress in a great wave that would meet no resistance.

What could he do?

He began to laugh, and even Ravengrim spared him a strange look. He must have appeared mad, but he had a plan now, and he would enact it. He was Kubodin, chief of the Two Ravens Clan. He had faced woe and destruction before, and lived. But live or die, he would not be cowed by any man, nor even demons.

He laid down his axe. He did not need it for what he was about to do. This was all him, and true to his nature and character. It was not the bravado and confidence of the magic in his weapon.

"Carry my words across both armies," he commanded Ravengrim.

The shaman gave no answer, but watched carefully and waited.

Kubodin looked around. He must act swiftly, for all about him he saw men trembling in fear, and some were fleeing the battlement.

"Halt!" he cried, and his voice boomed far out over the land and echoed back from the craggy heights behind the fortress. "You warriors that fight for your people, will you let demons unman you? Think! They are cowards for all

15

their power. Otherwise, they would have come against us in the flesh." He turned to the demons. "I know you and understand you, craven-hearted devils that you are. Do you know what I think of you? Do you? Let me show you!"

All gazes were upon him, even that of the demons, and they seemed taken aback. It might be that no human had ever spoken thus to them, and Kubodin laughed again to himself.

Slowly he turned his back upon the enemy, and then he unloosed the crude rope belt that held up his trousers. He let them fall to his knees, and bent over to expose his rear to the demons. He danced a little jig, awkward in his posture, and almost stumbled.

A deep silence had settled over the land, and it was suddenly broken by Ravengrim. The man laughed, and other warriors all over the rampart did so too. The bearing of buttocks at an enemy was a deadly insult, a derision of them in humiliating fashion. It had, in ancient times, showed utter contempt and there were several stories of heroes doing it in the time of Chen Fei. He had not seen it done himself though, and he wondered what Shar would have made of it. Certainly, she would have come up with a plan herself, but not likely this one.

It did not matter what she would have done. He had achieved his purpose in his own way, for all along the ramparts many men copied his act, and the sudden laughter from the defenders was like thunder.

Kubodin pulled up his trousers again, and tightened his rope belt. He looked straight at the enemy, and at the she-demon especially.

"Well, cowards? Come and get us if you dare, but live or die, win or lose, know that every one of us holds you in contempt."

The fear and despair among the men had dissipated. If the enemy were to win a victory here, they must do it by force of strength, and not by tricks of the mind.

The she-demon trembled, and Kubodin winked at her.

"Did you like that, dearie? Come get me if you can!"

He picked up his axe again, and it did not speak to him. Even so, he felt a mix of emotions from it. Admiration for his bravery, or perhaps for the purpose of his deed, was one. The other was disappointment. He had not succumbed to the temptation offered.

The day was young though, and even if he had worked a great shift in mood upon the men, they yet faced thirteen demons, a collection of shamans and a horde of Nagraks.

3. Too Much Power

The she-demon eyed Kubodin, and hatred was in her glance.

He had gone too far in directing his act of defiance specifically at her, and now he would pay the price for it. Death was promised in her fiery gaze, and even as he prepared for some stroke from her, she snatched the whip of shadow and fire from her companion.

Kubodin gripped tight his axe and crouched in a fighting stance. The whip lashed out, unfurling like a tongue of thunderous flame.

He did not back away, nor try to dodge. He lifted high his axe before him and thought of Shulu Gan. She it was who had forged the weapon in ages past, and by her great magic a demon was trapped inside, or had agreed to be so imprisoned as part of a bargain struck with her. At least according to some stories. Whatever the facts, he trusted that the demon must use its own magic to protect the wielder of the weapon when attacked by sorcery.

It occurred to him that such a situation as this, where no shaman but rather a demon was the attacker, had not been contemplated.

Death came to all men sooner or later, he muttered to himself. The whip flashed through the air. He felt a rush of heat, and then a wicked light leaped up from his axe to smash into the whip. There was a mighty crack. The whip recoiled in the she-demon's hand, and she staggered. The light from the axe, red and green mixed together, ran the length of the rope and down into the metal handle. There it flared, and screaming the demon let it fall.

Smoke coiled up from the she-demon's hand, and she lifted her head and wailed.

Kubodin barked out a laugh. "Come, my sweet! I see your passion for me is fiery hot!"

If he had not gone too far before, he had done so now. It was the other demons who acted though. The she-demon continued to scream out her pain and fury while the others cast magic at him.

Some spells came as fire. Some as ice. Wind was among them too, strong enough to topple giant trees, and there was envenomed air and the stench of disease and corruption. It was too much for one man, demon-trapped axe or not to defend against.

Yet Ravengrim must have anticipated this. He sent his own power, in the form of a flaring light from his staff, and reinforced no doubt by the rest of the Nahat, to crash into it.

The forces unloosed seemed to vibrate soundlessly through the air, and yet Kubodin felt the very tower on which he stood tremble. More magic was at work than he could see.

Even as the demons attacked, the defenders, given heart by Kubodin, gathered what weapons they could and drove an assault by missiles.

Arrows sped through the air, and spears and javelins went with them. Some even broke large rocks intended for throwing down at Nagraks climbing the wall, and hurled the shattered pieces at the demons. Those without weapons to throw cast their jeers.

The taloned demon of fire and shadow snatched up his whip from the ground where the she-demon had cast it aside, and he cracked it with a snarl of frustration that reached up into the highlands behind the fortress and returned as an echo of thunderous rage.

The demons ceased their attack, and they strode back some way until they were out of reach of arrow shot. There they conversed, and no doubt contemplated how their next assault would unfold. Without doubt, there would be one.

Kubodin studied them. They were unharmed, at least in any significant way. Some projectiles had passed through their defenses and struck them. They bled. That was good to know. They *could* be killed. It would take more than had happened now though. Perhaps if they ventured closer. Perhaps if the attacks were focused on their eyes. He sent word through an aide for that to be passed on to the defenders. What else could he do though? There must be something.

Ravengrim approached. Old man as he was, he stood straight and tall now. The fire of battle was in his eyes, and he had the calm appearance of a man not unused to fighting in desperate situations.

Surprisingly, the shaman bowed. "I see now why Shar left you in charge."

Kubodin shrugged at that. There was nothing for him to say, and he sensed the shaman had come to him for more than uttering idle compliments.

"This is a dangerous impasse," the shaman said. "The demons would rather not risk themselves in combat against an army. Nor can they back down."

"What will they do?"

It was the old man's turn to shrug. "They are demons. I know not. I only know that it will be bad. But the situation is worse than that."

"How?"

"Already great power is unleashed upon Alithoras, and confined to a small space. The shamans continue their spell, else the demons must be drawn back to the pit whence they came. The demons themselves cast magic at us, and the Nahat defy them. With magic. So much power in such a short time and space ... could erode the fabric of the world and unleash chaos. That is one of the reasons why what the shamans have done is forbidden."

"I see," Kubodin said. In truth, he did not fully understand.

"Nearly as bad," Ravengrim went on, "it need not come to that pass. The bonds that fasten reality to the universe will not give way all at once. Already we feel them tested, and they begin to weaken. As they do so the magic the shamans use to control the demons becomes less effective. The demons might break free of their control and fulfil their own purpose in the world, which will be worse by far than that of the shamans'. At that point, the gods might have to intercede, and a battle of gods and demons when the fabric of the world is already weak could be catastrophic."

Kubodin thought quickly. Soon, the demons would move to their next form of attack, whatever that might be. Yet in truth, they were not the enemy. The true enemy was the shamans who controlled them, and they were the safest enemy to fight. Their power could be contested without the risks to the universe that Ravengrim spoke of. Suddenly, he knew what to do.

"Ravengrim! Can you create a gateway something like the one that was used by Shar? Can you bring me to the rear of the enemy army where the shamans gather?"

The old man, his beard trembling in the breeze, thought but a moment.

"Yes."

"Then gather ten of your kind swiftly. That should be enough, with surprise, to do what we must do and not leave the fortress defenseless to the demons while we're gone."

Ravengrim spoke no word, nor did he move. He merely closed his eyes. Yet even so, Kubodin saw the closest Nahat on the ramparts race toward the tower on which he stood.

It did not take long for the Nahat to reach the tower. What Kubodin had guessed before was now proved, and he knew the Fifty could communicate over distance without speech.

Even as the last of those summoned arrived, Ravengrim glanced at Kubodin.

"I'm ready," he said, and he gripped tight the haft of his axe.

Ravengrim wasted no time. Light flared at the tip of his staff, and he commenced the spell. He did it somewhat differently from the Nahat who had created a gateway for Shar, but Kubodin knew when it was about to open, and prepared himself. Death and destruction were about to be unleashed, and he would be in the middle of them. All that remained to see was who would survive its end.

The gateway opened. The Nahat leaped through, and Kubodin followed. Even as he did so he glanced at the demons, and he saw their gazes upon the tower. They sensed the magic. What they could do about it, if anything, was unknowable.

Kubodin passed into the void, and mist was all about him. There were voices in it, but he had no chance to listen to what they said. Ravengrim, staff high and light flaring from the tip in a great stream, opened another gateway. Through this they leaped.

They did not come out near the shamans. Not quite, but they were close. A troop of warriors was between them, subchiefs and nobles of the Nagraks, Kubodin thought. He gave them no time to act. Instead, he used surprise and charged into them, axe swinging until blood spurted from severed limbs and screams rent the air.

The shamans turned and saw, but already a path was clear toward them, for the Nagraks had scattered.

Just as well for surprise. For the Nahat would not attack ordinary warriors. Yet they fanned out now behind Kubodin as he arrowed toward the shamans, who had been chanting but now faltered, axe swinging through the air before him to fend off any sorcery.

Sorcery there was. In moments the field became a battleground. Fire, ice, wind and smoke were hurled back and forth. Thunder rumbled in the mirky air, and the earth trembled. Back and forth magics were hurled, and Kubodin saw a Nahat fall, speared by a tongue of flame that gutted him like a sword.

Kubodin's axe fell. A shaman's head dropped to the ground. There were screams and cries, and the shamans retreated. The Nahat pursued them. Through a sudden gap in the smoke-ridden air Kubodin saw that more Nahat had fallen. Yet Ravengrim was still there, beard flying through the air and his face fierce.

Shamans had fallen too. Many of them. Then there were screams of terror, and Kubodin was confused. The screams came from the Nagrak army. He turned, and dread filled him.

The demons were coming. Like giants they strode through a field of wheat that was the Nagrak army. Warriors fled in all directions, crushing those that fell in their way and trampling them. The demons came, and wrath was in their eyes. They moved with haste.

Kubodin stepped to face them, axe before him, gripped by fingers turned to white. But Ravengrim grabbed hold of him and pulled him away.

"Stand back!"

"But—"

"Do as I say. Watch! They come not for us!"

Kubodin allowed himself to be led away. The shadow of a demon fell over him, but Ravengrim gripped his shoulder hard.

At last, Kubodin understood. He remembered the lore of demons told in stories. It played out before him now.

The demons reached down, and each snatched up a shaman that had summoned them from the pit. To the pit they returned, for the magic that constrained them had unraveled. Such was the lore of summoning, that if the magic failed, the life of the summoner was forfeit. It was offered in the spell as the bargain price.

In vain the shamans screamed, legs kicking and hands flinging fire. Nothing could save them from the dark spell they had wrought though. The demons sank into the very ground with their chosen prey, and for one terrible moment the she-demon looked at Kubodin, and her hatred fell over him as a shadow.

The demons were gone. It was suddenly quiet. Into that silence orders began to be barked by senior warriors, and the chaos that had erupted earlier showed signs of being fixed, if but slowly. Kubodin admired those men, for they had courage. Many others would have fled and never looked back.

Something hit Kubodin on the face, and he realized it was snow. Winter was here at last, and the enemy was in disarray. How long it would last, he was not sure. How long before the shamans regrouped, he could not say. But it must surely be a long while before they had the will to act again, and winter would sap morale as much as their recent defeats.

Kubodin turned to Ravengrim. Only the old man and one other of the Nahat survived.

"Get us out of here, old man. The fortress is saved for a while longer at least, but this is no place for us now."

Ravengrim opened a gateway, and they leaped into it. Looking back, Kubodin saw the shamans. Some were stunned. Others wailed. He had no pity for them. Then he saw movement from the corner of his eye.

4. Betrayal and Destruction

Despite news of rebellion, the abbot looked entirely calm. He gave no sign of the emotions that must be rushing through him. Nor did he give any sign that he would hand Shar over to the traitor Bai-Mai.

"What must be done, Master Kaan?" Asana asked.

"The temple is lost," the ancient abbot said.

"It cannot be," Asana replied.

"Do not worry, my son. This is ordained by fate. I have seen it. The temple is lost. Yet, as always, a new one will rise from the ashes. Such is the nature of our order. Shar must survive. We will flee, for we are outnumbered."

The old man made to walk toward the door, but Shar stopped him.

"We will fight for you, abbot. It is through me, if by accident, that this has come to pass. So we will fight for you."

The old man gazed at her, and his lips hinted at a strange smile.

"I appreciate that, but your death will accomplish nothing. Come! The way out will close soon. We must hurry."

Shar did not argue with him. She glanced at Asana, and he shook his head slightly. It was not a good feeling. She had miscalculated, and the advantage she sought had been lost. People would die because of her mistake, and from the dim sounds of battle coming up from below, they already were.

She did not like it, but there was nothing to do. They followed Master Kaan through the door and down the stairs. The fighting grew louder, and the clamor of steel against steel increased. There was smoke in the air too.

The abbot led them quickly, taking them through several turns and twists that would be hidden to someone unfamiliar with the temple. They soon came to the main hall.

The fighting was thick here, one side being pressed back by the greater number of their opponents. The tapestries that lined the walls were burning, and blood slicked the tiled floor.

Again, Shar spoke. "I can end this, abbot. Perhaps by fighting, and certainly by handing myself over."

The abbot did not look at her. His gaze was on the ruin that once was his home.

"No, my daughter. You are for other things. The land needs you."

"Then let me fight."

"No. I have seen that also, and it does not go well for you. Put regret and sadness aside. All things end, and great beauty springs from ruin. So it always shall be. It is the fate of humanity. Now, Bai-Mai will win. The temple shall burn, but in his triumph he will have only a handful of followers left. The people of Skultic will reject him, and his end will be a bad one."

The combatants saw them now, and the fighting intensified. A monk approached, one of those loyal to the abbot.

"What orders, master?"

"Retreat. Slowly fall back to the western exit, guarding Shar Fei as we go."

The monk went back to the warriors with that news, and with remarkable efficiency they worked as one to slowly surrender ground and move back to a doorway. The abbot led Shar and her companions there first, and they entered the narrow way. At least that could be easily defended, and the rebels would have a hard time of it.

It was a difficult retreat. The rebels were held at bay, yet at the same time the abbot had to maneuver through a maze of passages so Bei-Mei could not come up behind and corner the loyalists.

Each passage was tested first by a scout, cleared and then the retreat began anew. At length, they exited a hidden door in the temple and came out to open ground. The door was of sliding stone, and it seemed not even Bai-Mai knew of it, otherwise he would have had men waiting there. Asana seemed to know it though, for he knew how to open and close it. Most of all, he knew how to jam the mechanism that made it slide.

They were free, or so Shar thought.

"They'll break through in moments," Radatan said.

Already Shar could hear hammering and smashing from the other side. It was hard to see anything though, for it was the middle of the night and not a star was to be seen. Clouds hung heavy above, and the scent of snow was in the air.

A light sprang up. It came from inside the temple, and Shar realized it was fire.

"Nashwan Temple burns," the abbot said. He turned to Asana.

"There are only a handful of loyal monks left alive. You see them here. They are loyal to me, and I am grateful. But my time has come. They will follow you now. I give you the seal, and name you abbot. Lead them well!"

As Master Kaan spoke he handed Asana a small object. Shar thought it was a ring, but she could not be sure.

"Come with us, master. You might yet escape."

"No. It is my time, as it is the temple's. I'll not leave here. But you, and those with you, can start anew. You are the seed. Grow and prosper."

Asana made to argue, but the abbot stayed him. "Go! It is your destiny. Gather the Skultic tribes. They'll follow you, and Shar will have another army. Bai-Mai, they will shun. All is as it must be. Now go!"

5. Drink of My Blood

Asana knelt and kissed the old man's hand. It was a sign of deep respect, and one Shar had not seen him make before.

"Fly," the abbot said. "And remember Nashwan Temple."

The few who were left followed his command, led by Asana who now seemed possessed of a great haste. Perhaps, having been convinced to leave, he could not bear to be near when the end came. For surely Bai-Mai would put the abbot to death.

The wind blew cold through a patch of pines with a dim path. Asana took this, and by herself Shar did not think she would have found it. Asana went straight to it though. He knew it from a time past, however long ago it was that he had lived here.

Quickly the forest grew black as night, but the swordmaster led them without hesitation. The path wound uphill, and soon they came to a steep ridge. There the trees gave way.

Asana led them a little way farther, and then climbed a great boulder. Shar and Huigar joined him. Other boulders were nearby, and Boldgrim and the remaining monks, silent and subdued, clambered atop them.

The sight was heartbreaking. Fire had taken hold of Nashwan Temple now, engulfing it and sending a plume of dark smoke billowing into the gloomy sky. By the ruddy light of the fire, red and terrible as spilled blood, a swathe of the landscape could be seen, not least the doorway they had so recently used. There the abbot stood, old and frail.

And another figure gestured wildly at him, while a small group stood back and watched.

Shar reached out and touched Asana, but said no word.

Whatever argument was transpiring below soon ended. Bai-Mai struck out unexpectedly, sending a deadly punch at the old man's head that would kill him.

It did not. The abbot swayed back, poised and graceful, avoiding the blow. He returned the attack with a kick, swift and strong.

Bai-Mai jumped back, and the old man pursued him.

Shar held her breath. She could not believe how fast the abbot was, and he rained a succession of blows upon his much younger opponent. She began to hope the old man might survive, and several of his blows struck.

The rebel leader was forced back, but the blows seemed to have no influence over him. He bided his time for a few moments, and then delivered a spinning kick that slipped through the old man's defenses.

It was a terrible blow. The old man crumbled to the ground, yet even as he fell he rolled sideways and came to his feet in a swaying motion so as to be harder to hit.

Bei-Mei had the advantage now though, and he pursued it. He kicked and struck with fists and open-handed blows. Few landed, but one kick injured the old man's knee, and another struck him on the head.

The combatants circled. More words were spoken, but they could not be heard atop the boulders. It was too far even if there was no crackling and roaring of flame.

The rebel struck out again, this time hitting the abbot on the collar bone. The old man buckled. Bei-Mei stepped in close, and it looked like he was moving into some sort of wresting tactic. He was not. One hand was on one side of the abbot's head, and the other on the opposite. He gave a sudden jerk.

31

The old man crumbled to the ground, his neck broken. The fight was over, and the temple would be his bier for the wall began to collapse and the fiery timbers started falling down.

Asana sighed and bowed his head. His fist gripped the hilt of his sword though, and if ever a man could look dangerous in grief, it was the swordmaster now. Slowly, he raised his head.

Shar could not bear to look at him. Grief blanketed his features, and a terrible, cold anger. She could not look away though.

"Upon this sword," Asana said, "the blade handed down from my ancestors and infused with their spirits, I swear vengeance. Bai-Mai shall perish at my hand. I will kill him for what he has done, the betrayal of Nashwan Temple and the slaying of Master Kaan. It will be so, and I invoke the powers that form and substance the cosmos as my witnesses and oath keepers. It will be so, or I forfeit my life and my own sword shall drink of my blood."

It was a terrible oath, for it was not in vain. The swordmaster had locked himself in to the fulfillment of it by powers of magic, and they could not be denied. A cold light glimmered along the blade of the sword, and then flickered out.

Even Boldgrim seemed taken aback. He understood better than anyone the nature of such an oath, and the shaman turned his head away.

Down below the rebel leader must have given orders. There were twelve monks left, and he signaled eight of them into the forest. No doubt they sought their prey. The other three, and Bai-Mai, hurried away around the side of the fortress, probably looking to see what valuables could be saved from the fire.

"There are eight of us," Asana said, and his voice was cool again. "And Bei-Mei has sent eight to track us down and kill us. An even match, perhaps. Or maybe we are outpowered, for each of those monks might be my equal. Shall we fight, Shar, or escape to fight another day?"

6. A Well of Deception

A warrior came at Kubodin from the side, sword sweeping low.

By instinct, he hefted his axe to deflect the blow. He should not have done so.

The gateway vanished, and Kubodin remembered that a shaman could only hold one open momentarily. It was gone. With it, his means of escape. He was left behind in the midst of the vast enemy, and to die here would be the luckiest thing that could happen. If they captured and kept him alive, it would be worse. He had known torture in his youth, and he would never let that happen again.

With a roar he caught the sword with the spike at the head of his axe, and twisted to wrench it from his attacker's grasp. A backhanded blow followed, sending both the sword and the warrior's head flying.

There was no point dragging this out. The sooner he could fight, the sooner he could be killed by a simple sword thrust.

The shamans were still close though. He could yet do one last task for Shar's army, and try to kill some of them. That would inflict the most amount of damage on the enemy.

He yelled a battle cry of the Two Ravens Clan, and rushed toward them as though mad. Inside he was cold and calculating though. Already he was determining who among the shamans seemed the most senior, usually indicated by age, and he adjusted his course to head for a wizened man, his black hood cast back to show silvery hair.

The shaman saw him and raised both hands. Fire spurted, arcing between them as flashing death.

Kubodin dived and rolled. He came to his feet and saw nearby a sunken spot of earth, the turf at its edges smoldering.

Like a dart he shot forward, and he closed on the shaman before another sorcerous attack could be launched. The axe fell. Blood flowed. The shaman died, and lucky he could count himself for some of his companions had been snatched alive into the pit by demons. They deserved that fate for the summoning they had risked, and Kubodin felt his anger rise.

He would kill as many of these arrogant tyrants as he could. Wheeling, he darted at another. He was too slow to dive this time, and fire smashed into him.

With a thud he landed several paces back from where he had been. The axe in his hand glowed hot, and Kubodin had not even seen it save him, but it had.

He rose to his feet, groggy and unstable. All around him now the shamans gathered. He would be dead if they wanted him so, but they wished to take him prisoner.

That was not going to happen.

"I'll take you all with me!" he yelled, but even as he rushed forward a shaman waved his hand and a sudden wind blew dust in his eyes. Another hurled sleet at his feet, and he tripped and fell.

The shamans closed in.

Kubodin gripped his axe in one hand. In the other, he sought his dagger. Better to die by his own thrust than be taken prisoner.

He found the hilt and drew the blade, still trying to rise to his feet. He might take one more shaman with him before the end.

Even as he rose, there was a flash of light, and Ravengrim stepped out of a gateway nearby. He raised his

35

staff and sent a burst of scattered fire among the enemy, then he turned to Kubodin.

"Hurry!" the old man called.

Dizzy and staggering, Kubodin shuffled forward. He made the gateway as an arrow, fired by some soldier, hissed past his head. Then Ravengrim was beside him, closing the portal.

They came back to the tower. There, the other Nahat who had survived was having his injuries tended to. Blood was on his tunic, and a red welt ran along his shoulder and face where sorcery had lashed him.

Ravengrim showed no visible injury, but he staggered as the gateway closed. Whatever magic he had used in this task was great, and his face was deathly pale. Despite not being wounded, Kubodin instantly saw that he was in worse shape than his injured comrade, and his hand reached out to steady him. So too his heart, for the shaman had risked himself to rescue him.

"I will be fine," Ravengrim said.

Kubodin was not so sure, but he was distracted. A great cheer was coming up from all over the ramparts. The defenders were celebrating the demise of the demons and the bravery of the Nahat.

And brave they were. Whatever doubts anyone had ever had about the Nahat, they were dispelled now. Without them, the fortress would have fallen. Once more, Shar had proved her vision of what was required to fulfill her task was uncannily accurate. That, or she had the luck of the gods.

"What now, I wonder?" Kubodin whispered to himself. It had not really been posed as a question, but Ravengrim heard him.

"Now we wait. The demons are gone, and the shamans will think twice before daring something like that again.

But they are not destroyed, even if they must now be in disarray. They will regroup."

It seemed there would be no end to this war. No matter what the defenders did, the shamans would try something new to overcome them. Again, he admired Shar. She had foreseen all this, and that was why she had gone to the other side of the Cheng lands to raise an army. With two armies, and the shamans caught between, perhaps there could be some final outcome to this dispute. Perhaps.

"Whatever the shamans do, it's hard to see the Nagrak army attacking again."

Ravengrim nodded at that. "It will be a cruel winter for them, and men will die from cold and disease. But if they are still here come spring, then they will thirst for revenge. And they might have reinforcements to help them pursue it."

That seemed true enough, and Kubodin did not forget the advice over the next few days. It grew colder, and snow fell several times. The plainlands that had been turned to dust by the Nagraks was now powdered with snow, and there were not as many fires at night as there had been. Timber for fuel was becoming a scarce resource.

The shamans had much to contend with. Apart from all their other problems, logistics must now be a massive concern for them. Had they planned ahead for an overwintering siege? Or had they thought to take the fortress quickly?

If they had not planned before, they must be doing so at a rapid pace now. But every soldier that lost toes to frostbite, or died of cold or disease, would not just sap the morale of the army but turn discontent directly against those who led it – the chiefs and shamans. So while Ravengrim was right, and revenge might be on the minds of the Nagraks, it might lead to rebellion against their commanders rather than an attack against Chatchek Fortress.

It was too much to hope for, but all things were possible on earth and under heaven.

The days became quiet now, if ominous. The leaden skies were oppressive, and though the defenders had warmth and shelter indoors, rations were eked out in miserly fashion. There was enough, but this would make things last. Who knew how long the siege would continue?

Certainly, the siege was not broken despite the enemy setbacks. The Nagraks were there. Perhaps a few other minor tribes with them, and they showed no signs of leaving. Messengers were constantly going to and fro. It seemed that the Nagraks had, due to the vast size of their tribe, a group of sub chiefs that ruled beneath the auspices of the shamans. It was not an arrangement that helped them at times of war.

They seemed slow and ponderous to act, and must often debate among themselves until the shamans gave a ruling. But the shamans themselves were in the same situation. There were too many of them and Kubodin doubted they came to decisions easily.

Time moved slowly. Winter began to grip hard, and even by a fire in the fortress it could be cold. The Nagraks must surely be suffering in the open.

Kubodin did not change his habits. He spent the days, whether snowing, blowing sleet or crisp and clear atop the tower. Watching the enemy. Some plan was surely afoot, even if he could not see it.

Nahring joined him one morning, rubbing his hands together.

"You know that by coming here so regularly you make a target of yourself?"

"I do."

He glanced at Ravengrim who always shadowed him, and who now sat in a corner, arms resting on his staff that was laid over his legs. He trusted in that man now.

It was a day of ease, where nothing happened. Kubodin liked it. Every day brought Shar closer to her goal, and in the end that was the goal that could end this war for good. In the meantime, no one died, and that made it the best day of all.

He retired late that night to his rooms after having heard the daily reports of his commanders. Again, there was no news that disturbed him, but that in itself was disturbing. He knew in his bones the enemy were planning something, and it would be unexpected.

Even so, he was surprised when an aide, who also served as a guard at his door, knocked and came in during the middle of the night. He slept with the axe now, for he would not be parted from it. The shamans might send sorcery against him, and even if Ravengrim or another of the Nahat slept in the room opposite, it might not be close enough. He must rely on himself, and the axe, for protection.

The aide seemed surprised that he was such a light sleeper. Or that he came to his feet, axe in hand, the moment the door opened. If it were not surprise, it might have been a touch of fear.

"What is it?" Kubodin asked. He was wide awake now, and the dregs of sleep that often lingered with other people he threw off swiftly. Living as a fugitive, and traveling in foreign lands, had trained him to be so.

"A report has just come in that an attack on one of the fortress wells was attempted."

That was bad news, but not entirely unexpected. Both he and Shar had anticipated it.

"Did the attack succeed?"

"It's not clear yet. The report was vague, written in haste and brought here by messenger. All it said was that an attack had been made on the north well, and that several defenders were dead."

Kubodin thought quickly. Presumably the attack had failed, otherwise the message would not have been sent incomplete. But he could not be sure.

7. Treason is Afoot

Kubodin felt tiredness leave him like the clouds parting to show the sun. Finally, there was something for him to do.

"Quickly," he commanded the aide. "Have five soldiers meet me at the end of the corridor. Hurry!"

He did not waste any time himself. He put on his boots, took a sip of the watered wine by his bed, and left his room.

Almost he knocked on Ravengrim's door. But the old man must be sleeping, or he would have come out on hearing the aide talk to him. Better to let the shaman rest. He had earned it, and the enemy shamans could not know where he was if not in his room at this time of night, so they could not pose a danger to him. And he had the axe, after all.

Two soldiers were waiting at the end of the corridor, and three more arrived within moments. They had been quick enough, but Kubodin was in a hurry. The sooner he discovered what had happened at the well, the sooner he could issue whatever orders needed carrying out. Certainly, he must increase the guard even over and above what was already in place.

"Follow me, and be ready," he said.

The soldiers fell into single file behind him, and he raced down the stairs and into the larger rooms below. Chatchek had changed drastically since he had first seen it with Shar, but in the quiet of the night he almost thought he could see the ghosts again.

They left the main keep. There was a maze of narrow streets, if they could be called such, outside; killing grounds if an invading force made it past the rampart.

He knew the way, and he strode ahead confidently despite the dark. Even so, he took precautions. He drew his axe from the belt loop in his trousers, and gripped it tightly as he walked. It was hard to see, and though he was in a friendly fortress it was hard to cast aside old, and sensible, habits from other places and other times.

It was quiet. Almost unnaturally so. They were not quite at the northern well yet, but given that it had been attacked he would have thought there would be some sort of shouting in the distance.

The maze was confusing, but he was out of it now and on a straight path toward the well. Barracks rose to the right and left, several stories high. They were unused in this part of the fortress. Shar's army, large as it was, did not equal the size of the armies of the Shadowed Wars. It was puny by comparison.

They came to a crossroads between the barracks. The well was not far away now, but there was supposed to be a lantern here. If there was, some soldier had failed in his duty of lighting it. There was no breeze tonight that could have blown it out.

He walked ahead, and then paused. Some instinct rose up his spine and warned him. Something was out of place here. The soldiers paused behind him, uncertain. The closest one began to speak, but Kubodin grabbed him by the shoulder and pulled him down.

It was too late. An arrow hissed through the air. It flashed as a shadow past Kubodin, and he felt the invisible wind of it. Another struck the man he was holding in the neck, and he collapsed. Several more arrows hissed and whistled, and more soldiers went down. Arrows bounced and skidded along the cobbles of the crossroads, and then ceased.

The rush of oncoming boots was loud, and Kubodin rolled to his feet, axe ready. It was an ambush. Only two of his comrades rose with him. The others must be dead.

Out of the dark the attackers came, men with pale swords in the mirk, gleaming coldly, cloaked and hooded. Not warriors, but assassins. Not defenders of the fortress, but corrupted servants of the enemy. Inside the stronghold of Shar…

They were wary. Likely they had hoped the arrows would have done the deed for them, but luck had favored Kubodin there. He took advantage of it, rushing into their midst, axe swinging, hoping to scatter them.

It nearly worked. It would have if a few more of his men had survived the ambush. But they were too few now, and there seemed nearly a dozen opponents.

The axe crashed through an assassin's defenses. The enemy's sword clattered against cobbles, and blood spurted from a massive gash down his side. Kubodin was already moving to the next one.

Near him, one of his soldiers cried out, impaled on a blade and kicked away. Kubodin veered toward the killer, shoulder charging him and sending him sprawling even as he blocked a sudden blow by another attacker he had not seen in the dark.

It was a time of terror, fighting in the near dark and unsure who was friend or foe. Kubodin and the last soldier stood back to back, protecting themselves.

More men died. The enemy, warriors as they were, acting as assassins as they did, had no great skill. They were dangerous as a group, but their numbers thinned, they became even more wary.

The soldier at Kubodin's back cried out, and fell.

"Kill them for me, Kubodin. Kill them!"

43

They were the last words he spoke, but Kubodin did not think he died straight away. It was a stomach wound, and the relief of death would not be quick.

Anger rose in him. He strode into the enemy, heedless of defense and intent only on attack. Such was the ferocity of his charge that the remaining enemy scattered and fled.

He did not follow them. The energy drained from him, and he bent over and heaved for breath. Too late he heard a noise and spun around. One of the enemy had risen from the ground, and his sword drove forward. It took Kubodin as he was turning, and pierced clothes, skin and flesh. He cried out in sudden pain, but still his axe swept up and hacked into his attacker's body. The man went down, and his sword wrenched free of Kubodin at the same time.

Kubodin sank to his knees. Blood seeped from his wound. Too much, too fast. Yet he dropped a knee upon the chest of his enemy, and placed his axe over his throat.

"Why?" he asked through gritted teeth.

"Gold," the man answered. "More gold than I'd see in a lifetime, and less risk than fighting on the battlements."

Kubodin wanted more answers. Who was involved? How was it arranged? Who was in charge? Yet he would get none of them. The man was dying before his eyes from a wound to an artery that gushed blood in pulses.

"Less risk? You calculated poorly."

Even as he spoke Kubodin jerked the axe and cut the man's throat. Murder some would say. Mercy others would argue. He did not care.

He pulled a cloth from his pocket and stuffed it into his own wound. It burned like fire, and he felt the wetness of blood seep down to his trousers. He needed help, and fast. But the barracks nearby were empty, and the enemy might gather up their courage and return.

He shuffled over to the last comrade who had stood by him. The man was still alive.

"I killed them, son. They're dead."

He received no answer. There was a look of understanding in the eyes, and then the light passed from them.

Kubodin stood up, and leaned on his axe, the spike scraping against the cobbles. The closest help for him was at the north well. He might not be able to make it back to the main keep of the fortress. If the soldiers at the well had been killed though, he might find nobody at all. Or worse, the enemy.

There was only one thing to do, one gamble to take. He staggered away northward, and tried to ignore the pain that shot through him at each step. The pain was good. He knew he was still alive while he felt it. Should it subside, should he grow sleepy and tired, then he would have lost too much blood to live.

It seemed to take him forever. The dark beat in on him from all directions, hiding he knew not how many potential enemies. It did not matter that he imagined them. They *could* be there. Who was to say they were not?

Finally, he reached a spot he recognized even in the dark. It was a corner, marked by yet more empty barracks on one side and a collapsed structure on the other. The rubble had fallen into the narrow street, and there were broken fragments of pottery everywhere with the shattered tiles and walls.

Once it might have been an inn to the fortress, serving beer to the soldiers. Or a workshop of some kind manufacturing storage pots for oil and preserved foods. Whatever it was, he cursed it now. He tried to walk silently, but between the dark and his half-staggering gait he made more noise than a drunken reveler up to no good and too intoxicated to hide it. Each step seemed to disturb something. Each step announced his presence to those at the next street corner.

He held up the axe before him, but it began to get too heavy. It was a bad sign. Then he began to use it like a walking stick. The thought occurred to him to leave it behind so he could abandon its weight, but he rejected that idea violently.

The crossroads was in deep shadow, but on the other side were flickering lights and signs of movement. He paused, undecided.

There was nothing to do but go ahead. He did so, and out of the dark the well emerged. Torches burned around it, and there were a group of some twenty soldiers, standing at ease. Their quiet conversation drifted to him, but he could not pick out the words.

Suddenly, he was challenged. A man stepped out of the shadows that hugged the street corner.

"Who goes there?"

Kubodin studied him. The man's sword was drawn, but he seemed relaxed and comfortable. He did not look like a renegade warrior pouring poison into a well.

"Kubodin." It was the only answer he had the strength to give.

The soldier stepped closer, more wary now. He peered into Kubodin's face, and recognized him.

"Captain!" he turned and called out, and one of the men near the well strode over. He too peered carefully at Kubodin, and recognized him. He was a Two Raven's man.

"Chief? What are you doing here? Why are you by yourself?"

Kubodin leaned on the axe again, and breathed a sigh of relief.

"Has there been an attack here?"

"An attack? No, it's been perfectly quiet. Same as always."

It all fit into place. The message had been a ruse. The well was never the target, but Kubodin himself. The enemy had anticipated what he would do on receiving such a message as he had, and tried to kill him. They had nearly succeeded.

They *might* succeed, if he did not get help soon.

"Captain, I authorize you under my name to double the guard at this well, and at the others. Likewise, in those buildings where our food is stored. See to it by tomorrow at noon, and no later."

The captain looked at him strangely. It was not the usual chain of command.

"See also that a general guard is established to patrol areas of importance, looking for signs of trouble, and review our preparedness for fire. I fear a fire…"

At that point Kubodin grimaced and swayed. He could not hide his weakness any longer.

"Chief!" the captain called, concerned.

"Look at that!" the other soldier cried out. He pointed at Kubodin's boot, slick with blood. The wound had continued to bleed despite being stuffed with the cloth.

The captain began to turn to his men for help. Kubodin reached out and gripped his shoulder hard.

"No, captain. No one must know of this." He turned to the other soldier. "Swear to your silence. What has happened would be bad for morale if word got out. It would make people fear, and for nothing."

They did not want to. The captain urged immediate help from his men, but Kubodin commanded them, both as a chief and as the leader of Shar's army. They agreed, and swore to their silence.

"It's for the best," Kubodin said. "I'm stronger than I look. I'll survive, I think. But I'll need your help."

"What can we do then?" the captain asked.

"Get me back to the main keep. Get me to the Nahat. They'll be able to heal me better than anyone else. But I'll need help getting there."

He saw grave doubt on their faces, and he realized his wound was even worse than he had thought.

"Pick another four trusted men beside yourself, captain. Swear them to silence as well. They'll have a task to do."

The captain's reluctance was obvious. He wanted to call a healer to the well, and let Kubodin rest. He did as instructed though, whatever his misgivings. Kubodin noted him for future promotion – he was a good man.

They left the well, and Kubodin rejected all offers to help him walk. If the other guards saw him, rumors would spread through Chatchek like a wildfire. Already too many people knew too much.

The return journey was much harder than it had been to get to the well. As soon as he was out of sight of the guards, Kubodin's stamina deserted him, and he staggered. Only then did he accept help. The captain supported him on one side, and a soldier on the other.

They stopped briefly too. The captain insisted on seeing the wound, and when he did so he tended it himself.

"I have some skill at healing," he said. All he could do though was use more cloth to help stifle the bleeding.

They came to the crossroads where the ambush had been executed. Kubodin shuddered. He had new men with him now, and the attackers would likely be long gone. Even so, he knew only chance had saved him from being one of the corpses here, staring lifelessly up into the dark.

He spoke to the captain. "Give orders. Hide all these bodies, and erase all trace of a fight. Find a way to get them to the back of the battlements later where the dead are disposed of. Let no one discover what is happening. If word gets out of this betrayal, every man will fear his fellows. It's no way to defend a fortress."

He went ahead then with the captain and the other soldier who had first met him. Dizziness swamped him several times, and he began to doubt if he would reach the Nahat in time.

8. I'll Discover Your Secrets

Dusk cast shadows over the courtyard that formed the training ground of the nazram, and Shulu found a last patch of sunlight in which to stand.

The cold made her bones ache. She was not sure warmth made any difference though. In age, nothing did. Age was to be endured as were all other things in life.

If it were cold, the practicing warriors did not feel it. They were a good group of young men. A pity the training of the shamans would alter them, turn them and twist them. The nazram that would leave here would be infected with a sickness of the mind transmitted to them by the shamans.

They would see black as white. They would deny reality. They would serve the purposes of their masters, not seeing they were being used, as was the populace. They would believe people like Shar, who fought for truth, free will and prosperity, were the enemy. They would believe the very sins the shamans perpetrated were perpetrated instead by the opponents of the shamans.

That was how shamans worked. They did something wrong, and denied it. Instead, they claimed their enemies did it. And the people, blind to such manipulation because the hypocrisy was inconceivable, believed them.

Certainly not all. Perhaps not forever. There were times in the life of a nation where it could rise and throw off its oppressors, where it saw with a clear vision and took the necessary steps.

They were coming to such a time now. Shar was leading it. She was not alone though. Others helped her.

Others saw with her clarity, and their hearts beat with the same courage. A crossroads was coming, but what path the nation would choose to tread not even a great prophet could foretell.

It was not her choice to make. She would play, and was playing, the role fate assigned to her. It was the cycle of nature, and humanity, that at times evil rose to supremacy, and at others good. It was not her choice what times she lived in. Her choice was what side she took.

That was Shar's side. Always Shar's side, and the side of Chen Fei's line. There was hope in that. However much the shamans had tried to extinguish that bloodline, it yet lived. Chance? Perhaps. More likely fate. Neither good nor evil ever utterly prevailed. It was not possible. In the fall of Chen Fei and the rise of evil was the seed of the shamans' own destruction. It had laid dormant through years uncounted, but now it was growing. Should Shar succeed, then no doubt there would be an ember of evil somewhere that survived. It too would lie dormant until the right wind of fate blew it to life. So the circle would continue.

It was easy to be philosophical about these things when there was nothing to do, but Shulu sharpened her focus on the training warriors. They might be the enemy in the future, but right now their health was under her charge, and she watched them closely.

Already she had treated a range of minor injuries. Cuts, sprains and bruises were everyday events. She could look after them with her eyes blindfolded. A stabbing injury was far more dangerous though, and could kill swiftly even if only shallow. And such an injury was always possible. These men were good enough to train with naked steel when they sparred, and they sparred daily.

It was worse now. In the growing dusk it was harder to see, and accidents were likely. The training was necessary though. Warriors did not choose the time of day they must fight any more than a person, or shaman, chose the epoch in which they lived. They must be ready for anything that might come.

A warrior turned his ankle deflecting a blow, and that sparring contest was halted. The injured man beckoned Shulu over.

"It will swell up," Shulu told him. She had seen it happen and knew it was not a bad injury. Nevertheless, she had the man sit and she felt for broken bones and tested the range of motion of his joint.

"It hurts," he said.

"Of course it hurts. You'll need to rest tomorrow. After that, be doubly careful for at least a month. Once you've stretched the sinews, as you have now, they'll be liable to give way again."

"Can you give me something for the pain?"

Shulu rubbed her hands together. She let seep the smallest tendril of magic. No one would know but her. Even so, she looked around. Sure enough, she was being watched.

The previous witch-woman stood in the shadows of a pillar near the back entrance to the mansion. She was half hidden, and still. But Shulu saw her.

With a grunt of annoyance, Shulu let the magic die. She had taken the edge off the pain, and reduced the swelling that would otherwise have occurred.

She stood, and rummaged in her little bag for some herbs. Three leaves she found, dry and leathery, of a certain plant that offered relief against pain. Magic was better, but the herb was all that was needed.

"Chew on one of these now. Have the other before bed tonight, and the last at dawn tomorrow. The pain will subside."

"Thank you, old mother."

She shuffled back to the perimeter to watch again, and decided to talk to the previous witch-woman. It was time to make friends, if she could.

Moving along the colonnade in the deeper shadows, she came up behind the other woman. She had been observed though, all the way, and knew it. The woman she had replaced had not taken her eyes off her for a single moment.

"May we talk?" Shulu asked, taking on her most affable guise.

"If you wish."

It was a cold answer, and this was going to be hard work. It must be attempted though. The last thing Shulu needed was someone watching her.

"We got off on the wrong foot. Perhaps we can start again? I don't mean any disrespect to you, and I understand that you're upset at me taking your place. I do have the greater skill though. But if you like, I'll teach you."

It was an offer spoken from the heart. She would not teach any magic, but there was a great deal she could pass on in the way of herbs, knowledge and treatments that would be of great value.

The witch-woman narrowed her eyes. "You want to make friends, but that only makes me more suspicious. You're more than you seem. I don't trust you, and I want nothing to do with you. I'll discover your secret though, whatever it is. Your fall will be as swift as your rise. Mark my words."

Shulu smiled. She did not show her thoughts, for the other would have screamed had she known them. She needed killing for the good of the nation. What jeopardized Shulu herself jeopardized the quest for freedom from the shamans. It was a harsh thought, but it could not logically be argued against. Even so, Shulu put the thought aside. That was a slippery slope to walk. Moreover, the death of the witch-woman, no matter how innocent it was made to look, would only attract the attention of the shaman.

She tried again. "I'm but an old woman who has lived too long and seen much tragedy. I want nothing but opportunity for my granddaughter. If my skill is high, it's because I've learned from the best. I can teach you, if you like."

It hurt to make that offer twice. Knowledge was gained by sweat, blood and hardship. It was rarely given away easily, especially to the ungrateful or the unappreciative. Or in this case, the undesirable. Yet Shulu would keep her word and make this woman a great healer.

The witch-woman studied her, saying nothing. At length, she spat on the ground between them and walked away.

Shulu ground her teeth. In part, this was her fault. She had been abrupt at their first meeting, and then usurped the woman's place. Perhaps she could have done things better.

She watched the rest of the training session in a seething fury. Not only did she have a deadly enemy here who was watching her, it irked her to offer friendship only to have it rejected.

Full dark fell, and there were no more injuries. Still she stood where she was while the warriors packed up their equipment by the light of torches, and eventually dispersed.

Long into the night Shulu stayed where she was, silent and thoughtful. Murder was on her mind, but she held such thoughts off. Better not to be tempted by another meeting in some lonely corridor of the mansion with *that* woman.

The stars were bright. She knew them all, and their names. The constellations she knew also, and their meanings and influences. Not only that, what other names they had in different cultures across the land.

The stars were her friends. They gave power to magic, and the quality of their light, subtly different from one another, helped a shaman tap into the vast powers of the cosmos.

They gave her nothing now though. This evening, she was a bitter old woman who regretted her mistakes and hoped for more of herself than she could give.

With a sigh, she eventually left the now-lonely courtyard and headed inside. The servants' dinner in the communal hall would be finished. She would go hungry tonight, but it was of no significance. She had gone hungry in her life many times, through illness, ceremony or poverty.

Magic was her food anyway, her life and her spirit. She could feel it weaken as she aged, and she knew not even the longevity enchantments she had learned in her youth would be strong enough for much longer. Death was coming soon, and then she would be among the stars herself. She would return in the end to the place where she began, where even the earth had begun, and would return to dust in the great void.

It was dark in the mansion. Only here and there a lantern was lit, and she did not know all the twisted corridors and staircases well yet. Even so, she found the path to where she was going.

Already she was under suspicion, but she must take risks to help Shar. She went along a route that took her toward her own rooms, so she would have an excuse, but also one that took her through an area of the mansion where the shaman spent much time, and where his visitors came to speak to him.

It was even darker here than elsewhere. Perhaps the shaman was being frugal, or perhaps he preferred the dark. Dark hearts were attracted to their likeness. She should know.

The silence was loud in her ears, and she walked like a ghost to maintain it. For her, it was not hard. She weighed little, and was nothing more than skin, bones and a measureless mind that reached toward the stars. Sometimes she felt like she was already a ghost. Her body was not what it was, and time had wrecked it.

She passed through the corridors, walking slowly but not suspiciously. Her ears listened for any noise. Her eyes studied the shadows for guards. Her magic crept from her in soft tendrils, seeking wards.

There was nothing except the empty corridors of a mansion so large it could host an army. Until she heard, approaching a room like any other, the softest whisper of voices.

It seemed to her that the corridor was empty. Yet it was too dark to see its end. She eased to the side, coming up against the wall, and there she paused, her every sense straining.

The voices came again, muffled rather than whispered. Whoever spoke was in one of the rooms and not in the corridor. The door was shut, stifling sound.

Step by soft step, she moved closer. At the far end of the corridor a single lantern burned. She could see it clearly, but it was a long way ahead. In between the corridor was deep with shadows. Into the darkness she stepped, and straightaway sensed something.

A ward was in place. Like a string of magic it hovered in the air, invisible to all but a shaman. It could mean but one thing, and one alone. It was there to guard a conversation between a shaman and at least one other. It was a conversation the shaman did not want anyone to hear.

For that reason, she must listen. She must discover what was being said.

It was not a sophisticated ward. Shulu touched it with her own magic, and hid her presence as she moved gently forward. The shaman was capable of greater magic though. She could tell that just by looking at him, so she was suspicious.

Sure enough, she found another ward, much more subtle than the first. The first was merely a trap for the unwary, designed to lure them into thinking they had evaded detection, and to be less careful. Probably it was designed for the witch-woman, or someone like that. Certainly the shaman would detect anyone walking in the corridor though, whether they had the skill to discover the first ward or not. The second was meant for someone like her.

That was disturbing. Did he suspect her? Or, and this was certainly possible, he may be involved in some feud with another shaman.

She could not know. She did not really care. She had found the more dangerous ward, and eluded it too. Her only danger was a third that she had not detected, and that would alarm him.

There was nothing to do but go on, and this she did, one slow step at a time. If there were another ward, it was beyond her skill. She doubted the shaman had such proficiency, but her own powers were slipping. Once, she would have stepped ahead with supreme confidence. Now, a tiny sliver of doubt niggled at her.

To her right was a door. She could not see it in the dim light, but she could hear the voices a little louder from that direction. If the room inside were lit, it was only faintly.

No sliver of light showed through the gaps between door and frame.

With infinite care, she crossed to the other side of the corridor. Now, she could see the door, if but faintly. She pulled back her hair a little, pressed her ear against the timber, and listened.

"...the travesty is humiliating."

"So it is. It's beyond our remit, however. The war at Chatchek is not our concern."

There were some muffled sounds, perhaps a decanter being poured, and placed back on a table.

"Are we not shamans? All things are our concern, and Chatchek not least. It should have fallen long ago. Kubodin is a wily one, but that doesn't matter. It is incompetence, I tell you. Those in charge should climb Three Moon Mountain and never return."

Shulu breathed slowly. To climb Three Moon Mountain and not return was a euphemism for committing suicide among shamans. Things were not going well for the enemy at Chatchek Fortress. They knew, however, that Kubodin commanded there and not Shar. Whether or not they knew where she was now remained in doubt. Shulu hoped so.

Her heart sank as the conversation went on though, and she wanted to reach through the door and strangle the men inside until they spoke more plainly about what they knew.

"Not everything depends on Chatchek, and the shamans there know it."

"Of course. But a trap set for the girl is no excuse for them to fail."

They went on, but the sound was muffled, and perhaps they had stood and moved over to a window, and thus farther away from her. The girl could only be Shar. A trap was set for her, but what? It was tantalizing, and she was only *assuming* it was Shar. Yet if not Shar, who else?

She wanted to learn more, much more. But even as she pressed her ear harder against the door there was a noise. It did not come from inside.

A shadow flickered at the end of the corridor, and Shulu straightened. She had heard all she was going to hear of the shamans' conversation.

9. Noises in the Night

Shulu straightened and slipped a dagger into her hand. For her, magic was a far stronger weapon, but if she used it to defend herself the shamans nearby would sense her. With a blade, she at least had a chance of slitting someone's throat in silence.

The shadow approached. Whoever it was moved with greater stealth than someone who just happened to be passing down the corridor. Dagger in hand, Shulu still risked the smallest of magics. She just gathered the shadows to her. She would still be visible to anyone close enough to see her in the dark, but the shadows would break up her outline a little. It might be enough.

The figure approached, stealthy as a cat. Shulu did not think she had been detected yet, so why the stealth? Was it another person spying on the shamans?

Breathing slowly and gently so as not to give herself away by even the slightest sound, Shulu waited. If the newcomer intended to spy on the shamans, she knew she would be discovered. Whoever it was would come to the exact spot Shulu herself occupied by the door.

The figure did not though. It drew close, but stayed near the center of the hallway. Shulu ground her teeth. It was the witch-woman.

The woman paused close by, looking left and right in the dark. Some instinct warned her another person was here, and she sought them with her eyes. But by luck, or the skill of the shadow spell, that searching gaze passed right over Shulu and did not detect her. After a moment's hesitation, the witch-woman moved on.

This was a dangerous moment. The shamans inside would be warned of an intruder's presence by the wards. What would they do?

Shulu stayed still. She dreaded the shamans bursting through the door, but to move was to give herself away to the witch-woman. Yet it must not be uncommon for someone to pass through the corridor and trigger the wards. The shamans must surely meet here regularly. If so, they could detect by the magic that the person moved on and was not a spy.

So it proved. The witch-woman went ahead, even if slowly. Doubtless she was looking for Shulu, suspecting her of being the spy she was, and suspecting she would come here. Likewise, the shamans remained inside, although they now spoke not at all, or too softly to be heard.

Shulu's heart began to flutter. The strain was too much on her, and nearly she raced away. To do so was to trigger the wards as well as to alert the witch-woman to her presence though, even if she would now have the opportunity to escape down one of the many dark corridors.

Patience, old woman, Shulu said to herself. *You have learned it over the years, so use it now.*

At length, the witch-woman was lost to sight, though she might still be in the corridor. It was time to leave. Shulu knew she had learned enough this night. First, she now knew where the shaman sometimes met with his comrades. Second, that their attack against Chatchek was faltering. Third, a trap was set for Shar. It was enough for now. More than enough.

She crept away from the door, heading in the opposite direction of the witch-woman. She found and eluded more wards, and then turned the corner into another corridor. Only then did she hasten.

61

Her heart eased somewhat, and the sense of danger diminished by the time she reached her own room. Never had she felt so tired from doing nothing, and once more she knew that extreme age was catching up with her. It could not be escaped.

For a good while she looked out the window and breathed in the cool night air. It calmed her, and she began to grow sleepy.

Going to the bed, she made herself comfortable. But tired as she was, her mind kept working in circles. What trap had they set for Shar?

She wished now that she had held her nerve and listened longer, but that was not really being fair on herself. It was a stroke of good luck to hear what she had heard, and even better luck to escape the notice of the witch-woman. Likely, she would have returned that way, and there was no knowing how long that would have taken. The second time, the chances of escaping detection were next to nothing.

All that would have been achieved by staying longer was revealing herself, and then a battle with the shamans would have ensued. Winning it would do her little good. Her presence in Nagrak City would be given away, and shamans, nazram and assassins would all be searching for her without stint. She would learn nothing under those conditions, and all she could hope to do was try to escape the city and stay alive. That would be no help to Shar.

But what trap could be set for her granddaughter? Did they know she had traveled through the void and passed by gateway into Nahlim Forest? Did they know that now she was in Skultic?

Probably they did. It would have been unexpected though. Whatever trap they had set for her must have been arranged in a hurry. It would likely fail.

That was wishful thinking though. Shar was in danger, and she would be until the shamans were utterly defeated. They might be incompetent at times, but not always. Shar may have taken them by surprise, but perhaps not. If they had anticipated her in some way, then she was walking into a trap more deadly than any she had ever faced.

It was impossible to sleep, and the shaman tricks she used of deep breathing, meditation and visualization did not help.

The thought of Shar being killed, as Chen was, loomed up in the room over her as a shadow and sleep was impossible. She gave up, and let her mind drift over the possibilities of what she might do to protect the one she loved more than all else in the world. And the one the world needed just now more than all others.

There was a way to try to discover the trap. She could summon a god, and request that knowledge. Such an act was fraught with danger though. The god might not know the answer, or might choose not to tell. They could be capricious, even those who favored her.

Worse, she could not do it here. The shamans would sense the presence of a god, and they would come running to her room. They would know who she was.

Perhaps she could seek leave for a day or so, but she had only just started here. It would not be granted, and it would take a day or more to get far enough away from the city that she could have the privacy she needed.

There were no solutions to her problems. Not ones that were acceptable to her. It might be that Shar must just fend for herself. She was greatly capable, after all. She had strength of mind and of heart, and she had friends with her that were powerful.

Shulu turned over in the bed, hoping that sleep might finally come to her. At just that moment though her body stiffened in surprise and her senses stretched out. There had been a sound at the door.

She lay perfectly still. She heard nothing now. Had she been mistaken? It was hard to tell because she had been moving when she thought she heard the sound.

But the noise came again, and there was no mistake. Someone was turning the knob of the door. There were no locks, at least here on a servant's door. But Shulu had placed a chair against it. There was a moment's hesitation. Greater force was used, and the chair made a noise as its legs began to scrape across the wooden floor. Then suddenly the noise ceased.

A long time Shulu laid awake, silently staring through the dark at the door. Whoever it was must have got scared and given up.

But who was it? Possibly, the shaman was suspicious of her. Or it could have been a common thief. To Shulu's mind though, there was only one suspect. The witch-woman.

If it were her though, what did she intend? Perhaps she merely wanted to see if Shulu were there, or if she were wandering the halls and spying. Or maybe she intended some dark deed. Perhaps she had a knife.

Certainly, the witch-woman was capable of murder. Shulu knew that. She had learned to judge such things over long years of practice. But callous as the witch-woman was, and as strong as her motives were, she was not entirely stupid. If she intended murder, then suspicion would fall hard on her. She would not withstand questioning by the shaman, and surely, she must know that.

Uncertain and worried, Shulu eventually fell asleep. If another attempt were made, movement of the chair would wake her. She was a light sleeper. She did not think anything else would happen this night though.

She was right, and by dawn she was up again. She did not feel refreshed, but she was a shaman. She could endure lack of sleep.

10. You Have Failed

Olekhai took his time. He was in no rush to do what he must. Always, he had an uneasy feeling when he did this, and he was not quite sure why. Nothing scared him any more save the prospect of failing to lift the curse Shulu had cast upon him.

The room was dark, if it could be called a room. He had descended the pagoda and now knelt on the floor of the vault beneath it. It was more like a cave than a cellar or vault though.

It was hard to know where the building construction had finished and the cave began. For surely this place existed long before any habitation had been built here. It was a place of magic, and it would have seen use back into an age even before the Shadowed Wars.

The ceiling was nearly smooth, but he could still see chisel marks in the ancient stone. It was slick with a film of moisture. There was less on the stairs that gave entrance to the chamber on his left, but they were a little damp also. There were no chisel marks there. That was of newer and better construction.

The floor and walls were different. They appeared to be of natural stone, pitted by ancient erosion that no longer influenced it, and covered in slime.

Likewise, in the center of the floor stood a puddle of water. Certainly it was not man-made, despite the surroundings. And it was deeper than any ordinary puddle. It seemed more like a spring that welled up from far beneath, but nowadays it rarely showed much water. Once, he had found the crack up which the water rose.

He could not plumb its depth, but the rest, lying in a natural stone basin, was only a few inches deep.

It was enough. It was all that was needed for his purpose. The magic of this place did not rely on water, though water did offer a gateway between worlds. Even so, this place, as the ancients who first worshiped here when it was a cave knew, was a conjunction of great forces. The magic was strong.

Hesitantly, and he never did anything hesitantly and this therefore irked him, he removed the talisman that he had been given off his neck.

The chain was of fine silver, though it seemed heavy in his hand despite its string-like quality. The talisman itself, a horn, also made of silver, and fluted like a wild animal's such as a goat, was strangely light. Almost as though it were not a thing of this world at all. It was ghostly, if an inanimate object could be described as such. Always it disturbed him when he touched it, but he did not know why.

The talisman was the gift of a god. There was nothing to be feared in it. Rather, it was a sign of great favor. Even so...

It was of no matter. The talisman was his means of summoning the god, for he was not a shaman. He must borrow of its magic, whatever that magic was.

Gently, he let the horn fall until it disturbed the surface of the water. Slowly, he traced circles in the basin, moving from right to left. A while he continued thus, trying to empty his mind of thought and expectation. All that mattered was his presence, the horn, and that the god would answer his call.

Water dripped loudly now off the ceilings and walls. It was more than before. The room seemed to spin, or Olekhai grew dizzy. He was not sure which. Then out of the walls a thick fog seeped, cold and clammy, yet lit with a faint ruddy light as though it reflected unseen fires.

The god was come. The image of him wavered in the mist, at times blurred and at others stronger. It never seemed possible to see him clearly though.

Even so, Olekhai saw enough. The god stood, yet he was twice the height of a human, and his arms, corded with muscle, were folded in front of a barrel chest. A great neck thrust up from this, thick with muscle and popping with veins, but the head was less clear.

The eyes were bright though. They pierced the swirling fog and Olekhai felt transfixed. He was not some newcomer however, unused to the powers that shaped the world. He remained kneeling, as was proper, but he gazed back at the god without fear.

It was for a reason that he had summoned the god, and Olekhai was about to ask his questions, but the god spoke first, his voice cold as ice and nothing like his vaporish form.

"You have failed."

They were simple words, but the power in them would buckle an iron pillar. The judgement of the god seemed as a weight that would crush mountains.

Olekhai did not look away. "How so?"

"The witch, Shulu, yet walks the earth."

That was a shock. The tagayah had been sent at his request to destroy her, and a terrible creature such as that, from the Old World, did not fail. It was not his fault though. He had not summoned the creature and given it orders. Could he answer thus to the god whose fault it was, who had done these things and failed himself?

"How may I redress this fault?"

He had been a politician long ago, and the ways of that craft did not desert him. He could speak with subtlety when required, and to tell a lie while seeming to say true words. Or, as now, avoid provoking a response and yet not admit culpability either.

The god laughed, and Olekhai had the uncomfortable feeling his subtlety had been seen through, and that he was being mocked.

"You must continue to seek her death. She is dangerous to our cause. Kill her. Magic has failed, for she is protected by strange wards, or shielded in some manner by a god."

It seemed vague to Olekhai that one god did not know what protection another god offered. It troubled him, but the ways of gods were not the ways of men.

"If the tagayah has failed, what else can be done?"

"You should know better than most. You lead the Ahat, the assassin tribe. Send them after her. I care not if you send ten, or a hundred, or five hundred. Send what is required, and kill her."

It was an easy command to give, but the Ahat were not numerous, and they had other missions beside Shulu. Even so, he wanted her dead as much as the god did, perhaps even more. He could spare ten assassins, or more. It would be enough, if they found her.

"Where is she?"

The gods did not like to give direct answers to questions, at least according to the lore relating to them. Nevertheless, the stern figure before him answered crisply.

"She is in Nagrak City. So much my magic can discern, but no more. Send your killers to find her there, and on their success I shall honor them. But they must find her."

Nagrak City was massive, and it would be difficult. He already had more than enough assets there though. It was the center of power, and assassins were in demand to remove rivals.

He bowed his head in acquiescence, but it gave him time to think also. Of all places, what was Shulu doing in the one spot that was most dangerous to her in all the lands of the Cheng?

If he could discover that, he would know where to find her, and once and for all her meddling would be over.

"I will find her. Be assured of it."

The god looked down at him, and Olekhai felt the weight of a mind far superior to his own scrutinize him.

"I believe you. Yet I offer you this caution. Do not fail again, for limitless as the power of a god is, it is not so with their patience."

That was evidently a lie. If the power of a god were limitless, the one before him would not have bargained for help. Shulu would be dead already, and this conversation would not be taking place. It was something to remember. Gods suffered from vanity just as did humankind. Even so, it was not a trait the old stories gave often to them. Capriciousness, yes. Vanity, not so much.

He showed nothing of his thoughts. Once, he had attempted angering a god to see if death could be gained that way and Shulu's curse overcome. It had failed, but the experience had not been pleasant.

"What of Shar?" he asked. He did not like to say her full name. That brought back old memories that he tried often to forget.

"I know where she is. The shamans set a trap for her. If it succeeds, she will be dead, or their captive."

"Better that she is a captive," Olekhai said eagerly.

"Indeed. Yet the chances of the world are many, and no matter our plans events may throw them into the dust. This you know."

He did. He did not like it. For him, she must live and become emperor, at least for a while. But his plans were not the plans of the god, even if they worked together on most things. The god would have other options if this plan failed. There were no more for *him*, and he knew it.

The god looked sternly at him, and his eyes burned as fire. Then the figure dissipated, and the mist in the chamber condensed against the wall, dripping down the walls.

As always, Olekhai felt uncomfortable. He was not sure who this god was, only that he was a god. He dared not ask a name. He had tried once, and been rebuked. Nor did he fit the descriptions of any handed down in the lore. None of that mattered though. God he was, and he had proved helpful, not least with the tagayah. Even if that had failed.

How Shulu had survived being hunted by such a thing was beyond him. There was more going on here than he could see, and it irked him.

Her luck must surely run out soon though. He would send word to his assets in Nagrak City, and he would ponder what she was doing there. If he could fathom that, his servants would find and dispose of her quickly.

Shar was another matter, and a more important one. If she was at risk of being killed by the shamans, he must help her. If she were captured, he would release her.

It amused him that he was helping her, and her surprise at such a thing would amuse him more. Perhaps she had some inkling of it though from when one of his men had captured her. Perhaps. It paid not to underestimate her, for already she had proved herself an opponent to the shamans such as they had not faced in a thousand years. She might even beat them by herself, without his help. Maybe.

He rose, and put the talisman back around his neck. For a moment it seemed to catch as though choking him, but then it fell to dangle cold against his skin.

It was time to meditate, and to think deeply on what he had learned. Then he would adjust his plans as necessary.

11. We Will Fight Another Day

Shar felt her heart nearly burst for Asana. He had just witnessed the killing of a man who was like a father to him, and the betrayal of the Nashwan Temple, which had nurtured him.

She knew he wanted to fight. She understood he must bring retribution to Bei-Mei, in the name of justice. Or die.

Even so, there were greater needs than that at the moment. All they did must be for the Cheng Empire that could be. Everything must be turned to the overthrow of the shamans. Less than that was a betrayal in its own right. A betrayal of the Cheng people who thirsted for freedom.

She touched his arm, gently. "We will fight another day. For now, we must escape. For now, we must still try to gather the Skultic people to us as the abbot suggested." She paused, not removing her hand from his arm, but tightening her grip instead. "Even so, I have the strangest feeling that Master Kaan knew all that would transpire, and that in fulfilling our own quest we will also obtain justice for him. The two strands of fate are intertwined."

Asana did not seem surprised. Rather, he looked thoughtful.

"I think it is as you say. I'll not meet Bai-Mai this day, but I don't think the day of reckoning is far off."

They hastened away then. One of the monks, silent and grim, led them. None of the monks showed any emotion, yet Shar could sense their great anger at Bei-Mei coming off them in waves like heat from a furnace. The rebel's time of reckoning would come. But Shar had seen him fight, and she could not be sure that Asana would defeat him.

They traveled swiftly, and the monk who guided them knew all the quickest paths, and those that would best conceal their passage. How close the pursuit was, no one could be sure.

Nothing changed over the next few days. They did not see their pursuers, but they knew they must be there. The monks following knew this land as well as the one who led Shar's group.

Day blended into night. Night blended into day. The wind blew and stilled, and snow fell and ceased to fall. It was bad weather in which to travel, but the snow at least helped hide them. It only fell lightly, when it came, but it helped cover any signs of their passage.

The land helped too. It was mountain country, steep and rocky. The hard surfaces meant there was almost no sign of their passage anyway, and the snow covered the rest. Even so, it was not to be relied on.

Those who hunted them knew there were few paths that could be traversed at this time of year. If they had to make guesses at times, those guesses were likely correct.

Asana followed after the first monk, hood up, tall, oblivious to the cold. Shar shivered, more used to the mild winters of Tsarin Fen. She longed now for a fire beneath balmy skies and the smell of the swamp instead of a cold wind and snow.

When they rested, they could not light any fire except those rare times they found a deep cave. There, they risked it. The smoke was dispersed gradually through various outlets of the cave, making it harder to detect. More importantly, if they were found and attacked in such a place they held the advantage. The caves they chose were narrow mouthed and one or two people could defend them. The enemy, by contrast, must stand in the open, exposed to weather and missiles.

They did not have any bows and arrows, but one of the monks carried a sling, and he was good with it.

Asana brooded. It was not like him, but on the trail he looked neither left nor right, but merely down at his feet in thought. In the camp, he gazed silently into the dark, or the fire if there was one, in both cases his face a mask that hid his grief. And anger.

Often he took out the ring Master Kaan had given him. The seal of the abbot, apparently. Shar never saw it properly, and she did not ask to. It was Asana's business, and whether or not he would fulfill the role of abbot was his too. But when he took out that ring, the glint of death was in his eyes. It was not a good way to start a new monastery, and yet the abbot was wise and possessed foreknowledge. What had the old man known about Asana's future?

Eventually they began to descend from the high country. The snows eased, and the land was less steep. There were coniferous woods, and in these they found both shelter from the cold and a certain amount of food.

The monks excelled here, for they knew what tubers were good to eat, and even the few mushrooms that could be found in sheltered places. Of game, they saw little.

There were mountain goats, but they were wild and shunned people. Of deer, Shar saw no sign. Nor were there hares. It was a barren country, but no doubt there was more life here than they could see as they hastened along its stony paths, often looking behind them for the pursuit they knew was there.

On a morning though, clearer and warmer than any so far, they saw a column of smoke as they began their journey for the day.

"We come to more populated lands now," the monk who led them said. "Soon, there will be many people."

"But not yet," Asana said. "I smell a blizzard in the air."

The swordmaster was right. They spent the day traversing steep paths where rocky precipices plummeted far below. It was slow going, and the column of smoke was distant and much lower.

By nightfall, they did not seem closer. But the wind had picked up, clouds dulled the sky, and the cold air blew through them until even the monks, who never showed any sign of discomfort, began to shiver.

It seemed that Asana had been right, and a blizzard was coming on. They found a small cave in which to shelter. It faced east, toward the morning sun, and away from the cold wind that blew snow from the north.

There was some timber in the cave, prepared by whomever had last been here. Such was the way of the mountains. It was proper to leave firewood ready that might save a traveler's life.

Quickly, they hunted for what other timber might be around. Most of the deadwood they found was pine, which burned fast and cool and was inferior to hardwood. Yet they did find a dead oak sapling, which they hauled into the cave.

The fire blazed at first, and it gave off smoke that would be seen by any eyes that were around. Yet Shar thought the hunters would be preparing too. This was a cold shift in the weather, and it would likely be deadly if no shelter were found. The enemy would be mindful of that.

Slowly the cave heated up. Outside, the wind began to howl and a dark night fell, cold and terrible. They could not see much snow, except for a few flurries now and then that made it into the cave mouth, but on those few times they ventured outside momentarily, they came back in dusting it off their clothes hurriedly. It was falling thick and fast.

Boldgrim came back after one brisk venture outside, rubbing his hands together.

"We will be here for days," he said. "This is a full storm setting in. It will not dissipate quickly."

The monks did not disagree with him, and when Shar glanced at Asana she saw him nodding silently to himself while he fingered the ring Master Kaan had given him.

Shar did not know this type of storm well, nor the mountains. The weather here was strange to her, but she trusted the judgement of the others who lived here, or were better traveled than herself.

She did not like it. She hated the delay. She hated just doing nothing. She did not like the look of Asana either. What he needed now was to be out and about and occupied rather than penned up with his thoughts.

It was what it was, though.

They were careful with the firewood. Between what they had found here, and what they gathered themselves, they had a great deal. But if they stayed here for days, they would burn through it. If they ran out, they might even die of cold. So they kept the fire as small as possible, and were grateful that the cave was small and held the heat.

At the cave mouth, they set up a wall of snow at the base, topped by spare clothes to keep the heat in even better. Nevertheless, it grew cold inside while the wind howled as a demon outside during the dark nights.

Shar could almost feel sorry for her pursuers. They were out there somewhere in this, and no doubt they had found shelter too. But it was not likely to be as good as this. They would be suffering.

It was no great concern to her though. It would be best if they died of exposure, but she could not really wish that even on her enemies.

The days were cold and boring, and the nights worse. Yet, after a time, the howling wind quietened and the cold, by degrees, lessened.

They still had firewood, but they continued to use it sparingly. There would be little opportunity, or time, to replenish it as custom dictated when they left. So they did not wish to use it all.

That night the wind stilled, the snow ceased, and the temperature climbed higher. They made their preparations to leave next morning, all being well.

"What lands are ahead of us?" Shar asked one of the monks.

"Soon we will be in the easy lands. They're lower and flatter. The grass is greener for longer, and the herds grow fat. There will be villages. They will be friendly to us."

He said no more, but glanced at Asana.

Shar wondered what he would do. He was abbot now, and had the ring. Would he take up that mantle and use it to raise an army for her? Would the people respond to him? The monk seemed to think so, but he, like his two companions. Rarely spoke.

The next morning came. It was bright and sunny. Despite the thick snow everywhere, it was not particularly cold. Most of the preparations had been made the night before in anticipation, so it was that they left early to take up their journey once again.

It was difficult going. The paths were hidden, and the snow was deep and hard to trek through. It helped, somewhat, that they headed downhill. It was not long before the depth of snow decreased, for they were heading into lower lands, and the trail the monks followed, even if obscured, was well made in ages past and took a safe and swift route out of the mountains.

They rested at noon. Already travel was much easier, but they still faced at times steep slopes where the edge of the path dropped into an abyss. Or where an avalanche might easily be started.

They did not speak much. In the cave, in forced proximity, they had spoken a great deal. Now, free of it, and free of the life-threatening cold, it was as though being released from prison and they each felt excitement to be on the road again, and to enjoy the beauty of the view.

And the view pierced Shar to the heart. Behind them were the uplands they had traveled, mantled in white and majesty, and crowned by a pristine blue sky that was so bright it was hard to look upon. Around them were steep slopes and precipices, a few straggling trees and slides of barren rock. Below were lands where green forests marched, where streams ran, even if ice hardened their outer edges, and where fields and cultivated paddocks nestled among the contours of the land. It was the Great Wild and The Easy Lands as the ancient poets called them, joined one to the other in rare proximity.

They finished their meal and prepared to march. Radatan paused as they set out, and looked back.

"We are just in time," he said.

"Why?" Huigar asked, lingering near him.

Radatan gave no answer, but pointed up into the highlands.

Shar saw what he meant. There were figures there, too small and too far away to make out numbers, but she knew how many there were. Eight. They were the monks Bei-Mei set after them. They were the enemy, seen now for the first time since Master Kaan had been killed.

Asana stiffened. His hand was on his sword hilt, a burning light in his eyes.

Shar thought quickly. "They are where we were hours ago," she said. "They look close, but the path is rough going, even if we have trampled the snow for them. We'll be down in the lowlands soon, and they'll have a much harder time following us there."

12. A Trap

The travelers spent the rest of the day descending the steep slopes into the first vale below. When they entered it, they were surprised at the increased warmth, and there were patches of grass showing through the snow that was thin here.

"It's often so in Skultic," Asana said. "The mountains rage in winter, but the lower lands thrive. You'll find the tribes here, though far from prosperous, do better than many. The mountains provide a buffer that protects them from the wars, mischief and rivalries that hold back most of the Cheng tribes."

There was something of the old Asana in the way he spoke, something that had an air of dispassion, something that said, *I'm just saying the truth, whatever it is, and I do not judge it.* Yet there was a new note there too. There was a sense of responsibility. Shar knew without being told that he had made choices, and that he would fulfill the will of Master Kaan and become abbot. He would, in time, start a new monastery in memory of Nashwan Temple that was no more.

Late afternoon set in. Shadows crept down the valley sides, and the mountains glowed red behind them in the dying rays of the sun.

They came to a farm, and there the workers were gathered for the milking of their cattle inside a large barn. Asana entered first, and they looked up at him, surprised to see a warrior, and monks, and uncertain who the rest were. There was friendliness on their faces, but behind it, anxiety. They had no weapons, save shovels and pitchforks, near to hand. They were not used to strangers in this land.

Asana set them at ease. "We are friends, have no fear."

The farmers greeted them with hesitant handshakes, and commented that some were monks from the Nashwan Temple. How they knew, Shar was not sure, but the monks had a certain air to them, and the style of the swords they wore, and their simple robes and undyed cloaks, were different from the ordinary.

Asana held up his left hand, and the ring the abbot had given him was on it. The metal was not gold, nor expensive in any way. It looked like brass, and over the flattened top was an engraving, of a fist meeting a palm. It was the Cheng salute. It also symbolized, in warrior society, the governing of martial skill by consideration, peace and kindness.

The farmers recognized the ring, and bowed deeply.

"Where is Abbot Kaan?" one asked.

"Dead," replied Asana. "Murdered."

"It cannot be so!"

"Sadly, it *is* so," Asana told them. Then he informed them in simple truths of the rebellion at the temple, of Bei-Mei and of Shar. He did not mention that she was here, but it was not long before they noticed her violet eyes and the twin swords she carried.

"I summon the clans of Skultic to war," Asana finished. "Even in winter we fight, for our enemy does not rest, and neither shall we. For Shar Fei, and for freedom, we shall fight. Our army gathers on the low lands, between Skultic and the Nahlim Forest. Will you send word to the farms hereabout, and meet us there with your warriors?"

"We will," came the answer. They did not look like men eager for war. Nor did they look like those who shirked it. They did what they must according to what they thought was right, and Shar considered that only proper.

"I know you," one of the older men spoke.

Asana inclined his head.

"I remember you from long ago, and I've heard stories since. You're Asana Gan."

"Yes I am. But now I will become better known as just simply abbot."

The men whispered among themselves. Asana was known throughout all the land, and if they had not been disposed toward following the abbot's call to war before, they were now. Doubly so.

"The rebels follow us," Asana said. "Pick no quarrel with them, for they are dangerous. But remember it was they who rebelled, and their leader, Bei-Mei, who slew Master Kaan."

"We won't forget," the men said grimly.

Despite offers to spend the night in various farmsteads, Shar declined. She would not bring trouble to these people, and the monks who followed them might come here through the hours of darkness.

They continued their journey, despite the setting sun and a cold wind beginning to blow once more. They did accept provisions though, for these were always low and now they had more mouths to feed. Especially since the three monks that came with them had not had a chance to bring supplies of their own.

Night fell swiftly. The travelers kept going, wanting to put several miles between themselves and the village. The enemy were close behind, and the villagers were not expected to lie about their passing through, or the direction they left in.

For that reason, the monk who led them changed direction several times, abruptly walking up stony hillsides, turning into woods and being sure never to follow a beaten path.

It was deep into the night before they rested. They risked a fire, for it was cold. The light of it was diffused by the forest in which they camped, and should their pursuers be close enough to smell the smoke, they could not tell in which direction it came from in the still air.

Asana had a different mood to him now. He was as he had always been, but determination now sharpened his features. He had a goal. It was more than just helping Shar, and she did not mind that. He was helping her too, but he was beginning to fulfill his own purpose. He was making himself known to the inhabitants of Skultic, and taking on the role of abbot. From these people, he would slowly recruit more monks and build a new monastery. Where it would be, she was less sure. It need not be here. Once, monasteries existed all over the Cheng lands. Perhaps, under Asana, if the shamans were overthrown, they would do so again.

The night was uneventful. First light saw them traveling again, and they wound through the land going from farm to farm and village to village.

Asana always gave a similar speech, and the results were similar too. It would take time, but eventually another army would gather on the lowlands near Nahlim, and join the existing one there. Then, Shar would be strong enough to push eastward toward Chatchek. If things went well, she may be able to contact Kubodin and get him to push westward.

The shamans would be crushed between the forces she was raising, but it would take time. And there were many battles to go.

The days passed. Village after village and farm after farm came and went in endless succession. Of the monks that pursued them, they never saw a thing. Sometimes though, they heard they had been seen in a neighboring village.

Skultic was bigger than Shar supposed. There were multiple tribes here, but no one seemed to make much of a point of that. They were all from the Skultic Mountains, and they all revered the Nashwan Temple, and the abbots who had ruled it since the Shadowed Wars.

The monks often wandered this land, and they taught agriculture, wisdom, metallurgy, math and the lore of nature and the gods. They healed the sick, and advised in times of trouble. They worked for free, in field and households, and asked nothing but a place to sleep and simple meals. They never charged fees.

Shar admired them herself, the more she learned of them. And she began to understand the reverence in which they were held.

An army was gathering, and men were on the march. Already some had left, but the message Asana was speaking had not yet reached all Skultic. On the travelers went, and they brought it anew again and again to different regions. Yet, as autumn passed into winter, and winter turned onward from the solstice toward spring, a time came when rumor of them passed faster than they could walk, and they met troops of men already marching along the highland paths to the prearranged gathering spots.

It was different here than in other places. They did not even encounter shamans. For that matter, they met no chiefs either. This was a free people, and they intended to fight to keep it that way. All the more so since the Nashwan Temple had been destroyed. The abbot and the monks were in no small part responsible for the freedom here. They stood up to the shamans, and before the rebellion had great military strength. And a reputation that even the shamans must have feared.

It did not hurt that they were isolated by the mountains either. They were a natural barrier that protected them, but in the days to come that must change. A side must be chosen.

War was coming. No part of the Cheng lands could escape it. No person would go unscathed. War was like that. At least total war, which this was. The shamans would not stop until Shar was dead, the threat of her bloodline expunged off the face of the earth forever. And she would not stop until the shamans were overthrown and utterly defeated.

Only one side could win. The other would be purged. The fate of the empire would be decided for another thousand years.

She must be as ruthless as they. She must fight as hard as they. She must use the tools of war that she had learned, and use them better. In the end, there was no difference between her and the enemy. She did not like that, but she knew it.

There was one difference though, and on that she threw her mind to grip as a drowning man reaches for the shore. The shamans fought to maintain their power. She fought for the people, and not herself.

She would be happy to roam Tsarin Fen, hunting for food, collecting fruits and vegetables, living in a hut. She had no thirst for power.

Could her enemy say the same?

But once she obtained power. Once she became used to it, might she not become as they? Would she be a new tyrant, loved at first but then hated in after years?

It was something to ponder. But not now. For now, she must concentrate only on beating her enemy. And she was tired of running and hiding, of walking secret paths. And the burning in Asana's eyes when he thought no one was looking was an unintentional rebuke.

He wanted justice for Master Kaan. She was withholding it from him. No matter that they both knew it was for the greater good. But their task in Skultic was over now.

One morning after talking to a band of men moving northward in answer to the summons, she turned and spoke to the swordmaster.

"I'm tired of running," she said. "Of hiding and playing this game with those who seek us."

Asana looked at her, an eyebrow raised, but he said nothing.

"Our task is done in Skultic. It's time to make a start on yours. It's time to begin the process of justice."

"How so?" the swordmaster asked.

"By setting a trap for those who hunt us. They have great skill, but so do we. They think nothing of evil, and murder. It's fair to surprise them, if we can. After that, well, we'll either have justice or we won't. Either way, we'll have tried."

Again, Asana said nothing, but he smiled one of his rare smiles. So did all the others, except the three monks. They gripped tight their sword hilts, and the anger they had repressed nearly came to the surface. Woe to the enemy. There was death in their eyes, and justice demanded it. Mercy was all well and good, but some crimes demanded retribution.

It did not take them long to find a suitable place. They knew word of their presence where they were would soon spread. They never asked these small groups of men they met to conceal it from the monks. So the monks would soon hasten here.

On the right side there was a river, frozen over, or mostly so. Enough that no man would risk his life to cross it. On the left was a wood, dark with tall trees and choked with trackless snow. In the middle was a path, and here Asana waited, by himself.

The rest, Shar among them, hid in some nearby shrubs. The enemy would not be easily fooled, but they could not be sure it was a trap either.

13. Into the Pit!

The travelers had less time than they thought. By midday, the eight monks came into view, walking down the path.

Shar knew, even if by accident, she had made the right choice. If she had not set a trap now, it might soon have been the other way around. The monks were close on their trail. Too close to be by happenstance. They had known exactly where their quarry was.

"They look wary," Huigar murmured.

Well they should be. A figure sat cross-legged on the road before them, seemingly at peace, seemingly no threat. His hood was up, his head slightly bowed. Yet he did have a sword by his side. And what was he doing in the middle of the road?

The monks hesitated when they saw him. They spoke amongst each other, and there seemed to be some debate. Then they proceeded, swords drawn.

They came closer, and the figure did not move. In meditation he seemed, oblivious to the world around him.

"Who are you?" the lead monk called.

The figure gave no answer. He did not move.

Stepping a little closer, swords at the ready, the monks approached.

"Who are you!" the one in the lead called out, roughly.

This time the figure moved. In one smooth motion he came to his feet. It was graceful, but not threatening. He did not even touch the hilt of his sword. But it was an unwinding such as a snake did that was disturbed, and ready to attack those who trod near it.

"I am death," the figure answered.

For all that the voice was soft, it carried great menace.

Shar shivered. The monks would not back down. Nor would Asana. Blood would be spilled here, and death indeed would mark this spot.

"Is it you?" the monk asked.

"I am Asana Gan. Abbot of the new temple that shall be."

Asana threw back his hood, and gently drew his slender blade in his right hand. His left arm he raised, and the ring that was the seal of his high office gleamed in the cold light of the winter's day.

"I am your judge, and your executioner. You partook in the rebellion that saw the Nashwan Temple burn. You killed your brother monks who served our old master. You aided Bei-Mei to commit murder. Speak! Plead your case of innocence, and be judged. Or pray to the gods you serve, who will soon turn their backs upon you. You shall not enter their Halls of Light."

Again, Shar felt a shiver run through her. But if the monks were scared, they did not look it. Their skill was great, and perhaps they even felt eager to test themselves against a legend.

"We make no repentance," the opposite monk said. "And we recognize only Bei-Mei as abbot. His is the true line of inheritance, and not by blood but of time spent in the temple. He is the gatekeeper of our knowledge, and our ways, and our faith. In him we trust, and you are as nothing. You, we judge, and *you* we condemn to death."

The enemy spread out. Several of them eyed the bushes closely, guessing a trap was set. The monk crouching close to Shar sprung it. And he was right to do so. Better to start now than to wait until Asana was battling eight of the enemy.

The monk stood, his sling whirling, and a stone flew from it quicker than a loosed arrow. With a whir and a thud, it struck one of the enemy on the head.

The stone dropped down. The man staggered, his skull cracked. There was blood, and even from this distance Shar thought she saw the flash of white bone and brains. Then the man toppled.

Cries broke out everywhere, and the hiss of swords being drawn from scabbards was like a tempest.

Asana was quicker than them all. He raced like a deer, zigzagging into the enemy, springing from side to side. His sword flickered out, and it was like a striking snake. Two more men fell dead, but not the leader who had ducked and rolled when the stone had killed his companion.

For all the speed of Asana though, for all his skill, he faced men now who had been trained as he had. There would be no more easy kills.

Again the sling whirred, but the enemy avoided the missile this time. Even so, the other two monks with Shar, and Huigar and Radatan, had burst out of the bushes and raced at the foe.

They were not there yet. Asana was still by himself, and the advantage of surprise was drying up quickly. He could be killed, outnumbered as he was.

The enemy tried to contain him in a circle, but he was too quick for them, dodging and escaping as a fish eludes a net in the water.

They had to turn their attention away from Asana then, for the new threat was upon them. Shar made no noise, but the Swords of Dawn and Dusk gleamed before her. Huigar called out a battle cry of her tribe, and the others yelled wildly too. Even Boldgrim, who would not use magic against men, came forward, staff twirling before him. But he was silent.

The two groups met, and chaos broke out. Already blood covered the ground, and Shar knew there would be more.

She faced a monk, much taller than she. He drove at her with a swift stab. She darted to the side, deflected, and swung at him in turn.

With a deft motion, he turned her blade aside and attacked again. Instantly she realized she faced an opponent of enormous skill. He was as good as, or even better, than the Ahat she had faced in Tsarin Fen.

Backward and forward they moved, the battle around them forgotten. To think of anything else was to die, for their blades cut and thrust with skill that defied most training. They were masters of their craft. And their craft was death.

Yet the monk made a mistake. He was relaxed and fluid, yet not perfectly. He stiffened on deflecting blows that came at his head. And Shar noted that and used it against him.

She launched an overhand strike, and when he blocked it, she thrust with her second sword in the true attack. He had seen it coming. He moved to the side, trying to avoid it. But his stiffness slowed him, and her sword sunk into flesh, biting deep and then glancing off bone.

He was wounded, but not mortally so. He was no match for Shar now, and in just a few more moves she cut him down, slaying him without thought or remorse.

Instantly, she turned to the side. There Boldgrim battled a monk, his staff parrying, deflecting, thrusting, but never flaring with magic. She marveled at his skill, for shamans were renowned for being poor fighters with weapons. Not so the Fifty though, at least if he were representative of them.

She passed by Boldgrim's opponent, almost as an afterthought sweeping a blade out and beheading the monk from behind. There was no honor in a battle to the death where the fate of a nation rested on the outcome. There was only surviving. Or dying.

Nimbly she leaped over the corpse of a man Radatan had slain, his lifeblood staining the earth around him and his open eyes staring upward blankly. Ahead of her Huigar was taking on her opponent, but the man was trying to back away. Huigar was wounded. Blood showed on her arm and shoulder. But she was not beaten.

The monk knew he was though. His comrades had been felled around him, and now he was outnumbered. He would have turned and ran, except Huigar's sword would pierce his back.

Shar, coming up, twin swords flashing, was a distraction to the monk. One glance he gave her, one hundredth of a second of his concentration, but it killed him. Huigar used that distraction to drop a strike a little lower than he had been expecting. He jerked his sword lower to block it, but while he was doing that she smoothly reversed into an overhead blow that he was not quick enough to avoid. It cracked open his skull, and he fell, convulsing.

Only one monk was left of the attackers. It was he who had first spoken to Asana, and those two were locked in battle now, oblivious to all going on around them.

The others fell back. Some were wounded, but they ignored the blood that flowed from them. Instead, they watched the great contest play out before them.

And great it was. This monk was more skilled than the others. He was of a class equal to Asana, and their swords rang out over the silent waste in the music of death.

Neither showed fault, nor haste nor emotion. The swords slashed and jabbed. Sparks flew as steel deflected steel, and the metal sang like slender bells when struck with force. That was seldom, for both swordsmen were relaxed as silk curtains swaying in a breeze. They were of great skill, and astonishing force whipped through their blades with seemingly no effort.

Shar saw no sign, but by some mutual signal they agreed to a rest. The two men stepped back far enough that they might lower their swords. They did not take their eyes of each other.

"Half-blood scum," the monk said.

Shar recognized the taunt for what it was. A feeble attempt to draw emotion from Asana and make him act in haste. She knew it, and Asana knew it.

"A childish taunt? It did not work decades ago. Did you think it would now?"

"The truth always stings."

"The truth is a balm, if you have done nothing wrong. But you? You are a murderer. You betrayed your master. That stain on your soul is your fault, and it will never fade."

The test of character was returned, but the monk remained as unmoved as Asana.

"Bai-Mai is my master. He is the abbot."

Asana shook his head. He raised his hand, and the ring Master Kaan gave him glinted. "I am the abbot. You know it. All of Skultic knows it. Surrender to my justice, and I will show you mercy."

The monk shook his head in return. "When you are dead, I shall pluck that ring from your finger." He did not take his gaze off Asana. "And your friends will let me, for this is single combat. They cannot interfere, and as the victor they must let me go."

Shar was not so sure of that. It was the etiquette, but she might choose not to follow it. For Asana, there was much she would do. And the monks were a different matter also. One of them might claim the ring as his own, and the rules that governed monks were different from that which governed warriors.

Asana answered, his voice resolute. "You will not have the ring. I shall send you into the pit. And Bei-Mei I shall send after you."

Again, though no visible sign was given, their rest was ended by mutual agreement. They did not hasten, but stalked each other in circles, swords held in relaxed but firm grips, the points neither high nor low, their movements graceful as a cat's.

Out of nowhere they both launched a blistering attack. The speed shocked even Shar, and she knew she had been lucky her own opponent was not as skilled as the one Asana faced.

They came together in a deadly dance, and the music of steel resounded, then they parted only to come together again. Thus they continued, seemingly a match for each other.

There was blood down Asana's side. He paid no heed to it. A red welt showed along the monk's arm. He was oblivious to it. Again they leaped at each other, and then they parted.

For a moment they looked at one another, not breathing fast nor trembling despite the rush of their activity, and then the monk changed color. His face paled, and his knees buckled. He staggered to the ground, and only then Shar saw the blossoming of blood at his side. He had been stabbed, and the stroke had been too quick for her to even see.

The monk reached out toward Asana, hand open. Whether it was a sign asking for forgiveness, or a final gesture of hatred, Shar did not know. Then the man's head fell, and he died. The last of those who pursued them, but no doubt not the last to die.

Battle was coming again, and Shar knew it. The Skultic and Nahlim Forest tribes were about to join, but the enemy would now know of what was happening. What defense would they raise?

14. Beware the Twin Swords!

Shar felt a surge of pride. She was alive. All her companions were too. Against all odds, by the help of surprise, they had beaten their enemy.

More than beaten them. They had been annihilated. She surveyed the scene of death around her, and she was glad. Enemies must be crushed. Destroyed. Made into an example that would make other enemies fear to act.

Her thoughts were mirrored by the magic in the swords. They thrummed with power just now, having tasted blood. She felt the glee of that which was in them.

Then the world shifted. Perhaps the swords did not mirror her thoughts, but her thoughts mirrored that of the swords. The magic of them had crept into her mind and influenced her. Worse, she saw that Asana, victor though he was, had been wounded. And she had not even noticed.

Already the others were going to him, and they steadied him when he swayed on his feet. At Boldgrim's direction, they helped him to lie down.

Water was given to the swordmaster, and he drank. His hand trembled though. Only when Boldgrim examined him was it seen that the swordmaster had been stabbed. The wound was to his stomach, and little blood came from it. The sash Asana worse as a belt acted as a kind of bandage.

Boldgrim looked serious. He stood, and came to Shar, his eyes downcast.

"How bad is it?" she asked.

"Bad. Very bad. How he even fought with such a wound, I don't know."

"What can be done?"

"I will do what I can, but it is dangerous here. We are exposed to the weather. He needs shelter, and the warmth of a fire."

One of the monks spoke softly. "Not far from here," he gestured to their left, "beyond the wood and up the slope behind it is a small cave."

Shar took command. She rebuked herself for her earlier inattention, and was determined that her friend would receive the best treatment that could possibly be managed.

"Boldgrim," she asked, "can we carry him that far without risk?"

"Nothing is without risk. But here, in the open, he will not live long. I'll do what I can here to staunch the bleeding. After that, we must move quickly."

Shar gave quick orders. Materials were gathered from the nearby wood for a litter, and Boldgrim worked on Asana. The monks helped him, for it was the way of their order to study healing as well as killing. The first they used all through the mountains on their wanderings, and the second enabled them to do so, safe from bandits.

The litter was swiftly built. Shar herself took one end of the two poles, and another three helpers gently lifted their companion up.

They moved through the woods. It was warmer here, and more sheltered, but the monk promised the cave was not too distant. That would be a much better place.

Instantly they left the wood, the ground sloped upward. They climbed a hill, and wound around its other side when they neared its crest. There, some fifty feet below the very top, was the promised cave.

It was not large, which made it perfect. It would retain the warmth of a fire. Should Asana live until nightfall, that would be needed. Outside it would grow freezing cold.

There was no timber inside for a fire, but there was a ring of stones in the center of the cave where fires had been lit. It seemed that it had not been used for many years though.

They laid Asana down, and many of them went back to the little forest to collect firewood. Shar stayed with Boldgrim and assisted him to rebandage the swordmaster's wound. He used herbs from his own pouch, and others the monks had given him.

Asana did not look well. He was deathly pale, and he had lost a lot of blood. Boldgrim helped him drink water, which would help replenish blood. So too he made a broth when the fire was lit.

It was a subdued night. They no longer feared attack by the enemy. They marveled that they had defeated them so comprehensively, and yet there was a price for it. Many of them were wounded, though none seriously. Only Asana was at risk of dying, but the spirit that was in him was strong, and it fought. He often held the ring of the abbot to his lips, even when he drifted into a troubled sleep.

Shar remained awake. She stayed by her friend through the long hours, and Boldgrim remained awake with her. At some point in the late hours of the night, after midnight but well before the start of dawn, Asana stirred.

Boldgrim looked grave. "A fever takes him."

It was a bad sign. Even so, Shar had seen men live after a fever. The delirium worsened though.

Asana tossed and turned, and he began to mutter. At first Shar thought he had woken, but it was some strong dream that troubled him, and even in sleep he muttered words of regret.

Shar bent close to him in case he asked for help. She had trouble understanding the rambling words, but she caught a woman's name, and words of affection.

Immediately her mind went back to the apparition of the woman that had troubled Asana in the void. She did not doubt that he thought of her now, whoever she was, and whatever had happened.

"He slips deeper into delirium," Boldgrim whispered.

Shar knew it. She did not like it. Delirium often meant death. But not always.

She held the swordmaster's hand, and he clutched hers unknowingly. Boldgrim saw, and said nothing. There was a history between them, and a bond, that he did not fully know. But he understood.

The fire burned low, but the cave remained warm. The scent of smoke was strong, and in the ruddy light of glowing embers Shar saw it begin to swirl. She paid it no heed, at first.

Then she hissed. "Something is here."

Boldgrim had already sensed it. He stood, staff in hand, but not in a fighting position. He remained still, as though caught between surprise, apprehension and curiosity.

"It means us no harm," he whispered.

Shar sensed the same thing. She watched intently, not leaving Asana's side, still holding his hand. She saw the smoke in the cave flux and eddy, and then coalesce into the shape of a young woman, hooded and secretive.

She knew that apparition. It had helped before, and she lifted a hand in a gesture for Boldgrim to remain perfectly still.

The figure of smoke and shadow leaned in toward Asana. It whispered in his ear for several long moments, but what was said Shar could not hear.

The figure then straightened and looked straight at Shar.

The fire flared up, some lump of timber in it falling slightly, causing the ruddy light to brighten. Still, the face of the apparition was hidden. But its voice spoke again, only this time louder.

"Shar Fei, daughter of the line of Chen Fei, beware!" The figure towered up, but Shar felt no fear. This was the figure that had helped her several times, and whoever, or whatever, it was meant her no harm.

"Beware of what?"

"All things, for the evil in the world is turned against you. The shamans conspire. The gods are aloof, but their shadowy hands still move people as game pieces on a board. But there is one danger above all others."

"What is it?"

"The swords! The magic in them wakes. They have drunk of blood, and they grow stronger. They thirst for more. All the blood in all the world will not quench their thirst. Beware! That which is in them will strive to make you its tool."

The figure bowed then, lithe and graceful. The form seemed that of a young woman, but the power of the voice was one used to long years of command.

A breeze entered through the cave mouth. The fire flared again, and the smoke swirled once more. The figure dispersed, but the warning still seemed to hang in the air.

"You have strange benefactors, Shar Fei."

Boldgrim was not wrong, but strange or otherwise the warning was timely. The swords *were* growing stronger. She knew that. She must be on her guard.

Still holding Asana's hand, she looked down at him. He slept now, deeply and peacefully. Whatever purpose the apparition had, it was not just to warn her. It seemed likely that she had done something for Asana as well, and gratefulness filled Shar's heart.

The swordmaster survived the night. He woke next morning, tired and grim, but he could speak coherently, and the delirium was gone. By mid-morning, some of the local farmers had arrived, and with them came their wives. They were hesitant at first, but they soon became confident no harm would come to them.

They brought much needed food. To Asana they showed great deference, and wished him well. Many knelt and kissed the abbot's ring.

Apart from much needed supplies, they farmers also bought news. This part of Skultic was nearly empty now of men at warrior age. So too, the rumor went, was the rest of Skultic.

Shar knew she should be pleased, but she was not. It was true that she had gathered yet another army, or Asana had in her name, but she would only bring them battle, hardship and the risk of death. Husbands and wives such as these might lose their children, and it would be her fault.

It was well past time to be moving on. The army would be gathering now on the flat lands. It was her weapon, and much depended on it. Without her, it was more vulnerable though. The shamans might act against it, and if she were not there it might be destroyed.

Asana was in no position to travel though. Boldgrim declared to her in private now that he would live. There was no infection, and that he had been very lucky. That did not mean he could travel though, especially through mountain country in winter. He needed a few more days of rest, at the least.

She would give it to him. And if a horse or pony could be secured, she would obtain that, too. She needed him, and not just because of his fame as Asana Gan, and his standing now as abbot. She needed him because he was one of the few she trusted with her life, and she needed his friendship. Almost losing him had brought that home.

And there was the matter of the Swords of Dawn and Dusk too. Should the power of the demon in them start to shadow her mind, she trusted him to see it and take steps. It was a secret she trusted few others with.

15. As a Shadow

Shulu pulled away the chair that had blocked her door overnight. It was a simple thing, but effective. Magic was not the only way of doing things, nor, often, the best.

It was still very early in the morning. There was no sign of anyone in the corridor outside. For that matter, as she walked through the mansion, there was no one anywhere. It was still too early. Whatever activity there would be, was happening down below in the kitchens.

She did not go that way though. It was a good chance, while no one was around, to investigate the mansion as best she could. She did not expect to hear the shamans again, and even if she did she could not risk lingering in the corridor. The sun was coming up, and though still shadowy in the corridors, she could too easily be seen.

It was a chance though to see if the shamans kept any routine. If she discovered that, it might come in handy at another time when she was more willing to risk discovery.

Briskly she moved along the hallways, and she got to know her way around well. That might be useful one day should she ever be discovered and have to flee. She found all the concealed doors and narrow staircases that the servants used, and discovered many exits from the building apart from the well-used back and front doorways.

She also passed along the same corridor that she had crept through last night. The wards were gone. Even the door to the room was open. She thought of going inside, but there was small chance of discovering anything useful there. What she needed was information, and the shamans were unlikely to write that down, especially if it were important.

It might be a trap, too. She walked on briskly, so that if she were seen she could not be suspected of anything other than being a little lost in such a large mansion.

The household was beginning to stir now, and from time to time she was not alone in the corridors. She curtsied to anyone who looked senior to her, which was most, and acted haughty to those who were beneath her. It was not her way, but it was the manner of witch-women, and that was what she must appear to be at all costs.

Downstairs and in the back yard that served as an open training ground, there was little activity yet. That would change swiftly. If nothing else, the nazram here were trained diligently, and they were left little idle time to themselves.

Not all the back yard was devoted to a sanded training area. Like the mansion, it was very large. To the left, a row of flowering shrubs bordered the boundary. And yet the mansion extended beyond that. There must be more there that she had not discovered yet, if only a garden.

The shrubs were not in flower now, for winter was biting hard. They looked a bit tattered, but she did not doubt, come spring, they would be well manicured and lush with flowers. The shaman here had wealth, and apart from all else he employed several groundskeepers.

Shulu came to the shrubs. They were solid like a hedge, yet near the mansion was a wicker gate, twined with the tendrils of some half-dead vine. It too would burst into life come spring.

The gate was latched, but not locked. There was no reason she should not enter. It did not seem the type of place people were allowed to go to without good reason though. Even so, she was new. She had an excuse of not knowing and of wanting to get to know the grounds. And it was not locked.

She opened the gate and passed to the other side, closing it behind her noiselessly. The hinges were well oiled. Everything in the compound was of the finest materials, and well maintained. How many peasants toiled in backbreaking labor, barely able to put food on the table in order to pay for it all?

She was not surprised by what she saw on the other side. It was a garden of intricate design. There were stone-paved paths through aisles of trees, and small ponds where colored fish darted and ducks swam. Here, even in winter, the water would not freeze over. It was a sheltered spot, and high brick walls surrounded it all, helping to keep warmth in and cold winds out.

Shulu followed a path. She walked quietly, hugging the sides. Here, in the garden, there were still plenty of shadows because of the tall walls and taller trees. In one place she found several workmen pruning a tree and planting some kind of bulb in a nearby bed. She skirted around them, choosing a path that would hide her.

There were no other workmen. However, just as she came to the far wall and was about to retrace her steps, she discovered an outdoor pagoda. It was small and quaint, its roof colorfully painted and with a bridge over a pond leading to the front door.

None of that really attracted her attention. What did was the two guards standing at the front of the bridge. What need did a pagoda in a garden have for protection?

Shulu thought quickly. It was one thing to be caught wandering the garden, but it was another to try to sneak around those guards and see what was happening in the pagoda. For the first, she had a plausible, if suspicious excuse. For the second…

She made up her mind regardless. She must discover more of what was happening, if she could. And though the pagoda was guarded, it seemed there was an approach via some bushes that might hide her.

16. Dangerous Magic

Shulu crept forward. If she were seen, it would be obvious that she was spying. She did not plan on being seen though.

A touch of her magic winged out with a prayer from her lips, and a shadow draped around her. It was a small sorcery. It would not fool anyone who looked closely, but it was enough to help deceive a passing glance.

As she crept forward, she kept to the deeper shadows too, and paused at times to listen for signs of anyone she could not see. The garden was both her friend and foe. So many plants helped conceal her. Yet so too they might conceal another guard, or group of guards, beside the two at the little bridge.

Luck seemed to be with her. She was close now, and had discovered no one else. The two guards stood to attention, close now, and she moved around them, concealed by a line of shrubs, and came to the back of the pagoda.

Not everything was to her advantage. The pagoda was surrounded by a moat, if a narrow and shallow one. It would be easy to wade through, but it would be much harder to do so without noise. And though the guards were now out of sight on the other side of the building, they were still within earshot of all but a soft noise.

Not only that, if she got her clothes wet, it would be hard to explain. Moving carefully, she circled around a little farther. There was a tree, of what kind she could not tell for all its leaves had fallen, but the bare branches spread out in a crown, and though none were large, she was not heavy.

Nimbly, she climbed the tree. If the shamans saw her now, they would laugh. She was slight as a little girl, and from a distance might be taken as such. Woe to them if they discovered her though.

They did not. Ascending the trunk and then slowly moving out along a branch, she dropped silently to the ground. There she waited, catching her breath.

Time was pressing. The sun had fully risen, and she should expect more people around who might see her.

The mound around the base of the pagoda was smooth grass, and she stepped forward lightly, then stopped mid stride.

There was a ward. She recognized the touch of its maker. It was the same shaman as last night, and that gave her hope. Her efforts here were not wasted. By the luck of the gods, or by chance, she had stumbled upon another meeting place, and no doubt matters of import were being discussed inside.

She bypassed the ward. Immediately, she found another, much more subtle. It was just as last night, and she negated it too. There was a window in sight now, and she bent low.

There was little chance of being seen from inside. A bush grew near the window, blocking most of the view. No doubt it would be trimmed shortly, ready for a flush of spring flowers, but for now it served her purpose admirably.

On hands and knees, she crept up to it, and beyond. Her head was below the sill of the window. She heard nothing though, but dared not risk lifting her head for a look inside. She had already ridden her luck as far as she felt she could.

There she waited, and soon she did hear voices. They were very loud, and she realized the speakers must be sitting close to the window. The lack of sound before had just been a long pause in conversation.

It was the same men as last night, and the shaman who employed her was the one talking.

"It failed. What more can be said than that?"

"It failed *this* time," came the reply.

There was another long pause. "Do you think they might attempt it again?"

Her master, or such at least he thought himself, sounded incredulous.

"Why not? All magic requires practice. If it does not work the first time, then by trial and error the way forward will be found. How else did Shulu discover it in the first place?"

Her master muttered something she could not catch, and a shiver went up Shulu's spine. They were talking of her, and the irony of the situation should have been amusing. Instead, she felt a stab of fear. What magic had she mastered that they might try now? There could be several, but she feared the worst.

"There won't be any of us left alive, if we're forced to keep experimenting with *that* kind of magic."

"You're too timid," came the reply of the second voice. "Demons can be controlled. They almost had it right the first time."

"Almost isn't good enough. They died, or worse. Some were snatched alive down into the pit when the magic failed. And Chatchek Fortress still stands."

So that was it. Shulu leaned against the stone wall of the pagoda, feeling every century of her age. The shamans had summoned demons to destroy Chatchek, and in turn had been killed themselves. Serves them right. The magic was beyond them. It was beyond even her, except in limited ways. Even she would not attempt again what she had achieved in her youth. The dangers were indescribable, and not just to those who invoked the magic. All Alithoras could pay for their blunders. Fools that they were though, they might continue.

It told her something though. Stupid as the shamans were, hungry for power as they had always been, they must be *desperate* to attempt such magic. Shar was getting to them. She was eating away at their confidence and haunting their dreams. She was everything they hoped destroyed long ago, and the one thing that could topple them into catastrophic ruin. They hated her. They feared her. They would do anything, risk everything, to destroy her.

What they did now was dangerous for them and the land. Dangerous beyond thought. Yet if they somehow succeeded, it would be worse for Shar.

Something was wrong though. She could not pinpoint it at first. The shamans kept talking, but suddenly they shifted to the weather. Why would they do that? It was disturbing.

Shulu felt a pang of fear. Had they detected her? It was possible. That would explain why they spoke of matters of no importance. Whatever the case, it was time to leave, and to leave quickly. Her luck had been good, and she felt it must run out soon. No string of good luck ever lasted without being turned to bad in the end, and the other way around, for that matter.

She took her weight off the wall and prepared to turn. At that moment her hair stood on end, a sure sign of great magic close at hand, and then something smashed into her.

Her body thudded against the wall of the pagoda, and she felt something pin her down. She could not see, for her head was pressed against the bricks. Whatever it was had tremendous strength. It made no noise though.

17. Like an Evil Shadow

Shulu felt the air squeezed from her, and the brittle bones of her ribs were near to breaking.

Worse, the shamans were silent. They could not have failed to hear the commotion, if they had not sensed something earlier, so they were coming for her too.

She fought back. With all her strength she heaved against whatever pinned her down. But it was too strong for her. Too strong by far.

Magic flared to life within her. Nothing less would save her now, and if the shamans sensed it blossoming, that could not be helped.

Fire rippled from her body. It spread outward but had no influence over the creature at all. It did not jump away, nor snarl, nor lash out. It remained utterly unchanged.

Stupid! So stupid! Shulu cursed herself. This was not a creature of flesh. It was a ward of magic that she had not detected, but it had detected her. Probably when she touched the wall of the pagoda. It was binding her. Holding her prisoner. It was there to trap her until the shamans arrived, and that must only be a matter of seconds away.

Now that she understood her enemy, she knew better how to fight it. Her magic leaped up again, but this time it did not attack.

Quick as a flash of light it leaped out, finding the ward, and then traced it back to its source: the shaman who had created it.

The sorcery was of many threads. Some elements were to hide it. Others to sense the approach of any person, yet others still were what she felt now – the binding power. All in all, it was remarkably sophisticated, and her admiration of the shaman went up. It was a highly skillful trap. And it was too complex to unweave and disengage.

There was another method that would serve. Brute force. But destroying a ward such as this outright would reveal the presence of a powerful shaman. None other could do so, and that was dangerous.

The enemy would know that a shaman was spying on them. Who else would it be but Shulu? And that would draw suspicion onto her as the witch-woman. Still, it could be a member of the Nahat, operating at Shar's instructions. They might be inclined to think that too.

No time was left to her. She lashed out with great strength, her magic rending the ward to shreds. It was not easy. Some shamans would not have the strength to do so, but she was Shulu Gan, and she was becoming desperate.

There was a flash of many-hued light. To add to that, she muttered a spell and drew smoke up from the earth to help conceal her.

It was none too soon. She heard the tread of boots, and the two guards from the bridge were there, swords drawn. Behind them were several shamans. There were more there than she had heard. Among them was the master of the house, and one other whom she recognized of old. He had lived during Chen Fei's time, and he would recognize her if he saw her. At least, he would be suspicious given the power she had used to destroy the ward.

With a gesture, she brought more smoke forth. It billowed up, covering her completely. She did not think the shamans had seen her.

Leaping to the branch, she clambered across to the other side of the moat and dropped down.

There was some shouting, and a splash of water near her. The guards had entered the moat.

Muttering as she ran, Shulu drew up more smoke, and sent flashes of light scattering across the garden. That should conceal her and confuse the pursuit.

The result was not quite what she anticipated. The enemy, not seeing her, sent bolts of magic hurtling through the air. With a roar and mighty crash, the wall was hit in several places. Trees burst into flame, igniting like candles with green and crimson flames licking up from their tops.

The wall was hit behind her, and with a massive heave of stone that section tumbled down. Quick as thought, Shulu doubled back. She clambered over the rubble and came to the footpath at the front road.

It was the safest place to be, if they had not seen her go there. The wall would protect her from attack. It would hide her too. She raced ahead, coming to the front of the mansion.

A quick turn and glance told her the ruse had worked. There was no more sorcery unleashed blindly inside the garden, but likewise no one else had clambered through the gap in the wall. Nor was there anyone on the street at this time of day.

She made a quick decision. Suspicion would fall to her as a newcomer, but they had not seen her. She slipped into the mansion again, not using the main entrance but one of the small servant doors.

The corridor was narrow, but empty. Quickly she strode down it, took a few turns and made her way back to her own room.

Several times she heard people coming, and slipped backward to take another turn. She did not wish to be seen. Even inside the mansion, that could only add to any suspicion that might fall on her.

It did not take too long. There were not many people about, either because the hour was still early or because many had been drawn to the side of the mansion to look out the windows. The havoc in the garden would certainly be drawing gazes.

To her great surprise, the door to her room was open. That was not how she had left it.

She crept close. Had the shamans somehow identified her? Was she walking into a trap? If so, how had they reached here before her?

She could be sure of nothing. The only way to discover the truth was to move forward. There was no one in the corridor, so she moved ahead on cat's feet. She summoned up her magic until it nearly burst from her. There might be several shamans inside, and she would not be taken alive. Better to die, or kill them all and flee.

There was a noise from inside. Shulu peeked around the edge of the open door, and fury welled within her. It was the witch-woman, and she was going through the draws to the small wardrobe in the corner.

Shulu felt her anger rise even further. Always this woman was in the way. She felt an urge to rend and destroy, to unleash her power and finish off this meddler once and for all.

Instead, she let her magic subside and crept away. It was not the way of shamans to use magic against those who could not defend themselves in a like manner. It was true the witch-woman possessed some magic of her own, but it was next to nothing.

Moreover, the death of the woman in her room would never be able to be explained away. No, it was better to go elsewhere. Where could she go that might support an alibi for her?

She thought of one place, but it was dangerous. No better options were open to her though.

116

Quickly, and avoiding any encounters with anyone, she passed through the corridors and went downstairs to the training area at the back of the mansion. No one was practicing. They were gathered in groups and talking of this morning's events. Shulu could still see the tops of some trees smoldering.

She pushed ahead, sticking to the shadows along the colonnade at the back of the building, drawing some more shadows about her with a touch of magic, and praying to the gods that no one would see her.

It was possible that if she were questioned, she could say that she had been here all along. But there were many potential witnesses here, and if she appeared now all would say it was only after the commotion in the garden. If she held back and stayed hidden in the colonnade, she could make the same claim, but it would seem strange that no one had seen her at all during that length of time.

There was a better place to be, and she headed for it. Again, being careful not to be seen, she moved over to the smaller building on the far side where she had first been brought by the shaman. There she found the room of the man she had healed.

The warrior was asleep, but he looked well. No one else was there, and she pulled a chair close to his bed and sat down. Here she would stay until she was seen, and here she would claim to have been all along if anyone asked.

It was gratifying to see that her efforts had been rewarded. The man before her had faced certain death. She had saved him, even at risk to herself. She quickly turned her mind to other matters though, thinking through the events of the morning and what she had learned.

It did not seem long at all though before she felt a shadow pass over the threshold of the room. Someone had entered. She turned, and was surprised to see it was the shaman himself. With him was the witch-woman, and once again Shulu felt anger overtake her.

"As I told you, master, she was not in her room. What is she doing here, with a well man?"

The shaman scrutinized her, and his gaze was harsh. Suspicion was in it, but doubt also. Someone had been spying on him, someone of power as great as his own, and he did not like it. Not one bit.

"Well?" he asked. "You were not in your room, nor in the training yard. Explain yourself."

Shulu bowed her head meekly. But her answer was anything but.

"Where else should I be? This man was dying when I came here. I healed him. Is it not proper that I check on his progress? That's what you pay me for, is it not?"

The shaman's gaze hardened. Then it shifted away from Shulu to the man on the bed.

"Is it true? Has she been here for some while?"

Shulu had not known, but the warrior was now awake. This was a moment of great danger, and she felt her magic begin to stir. She suppressed it. The time for fighting was not yet come.

"She has been here quite a while. I was dozing when she came in, but it was at dawn."

Shulu did not look at him. She held herself still to keep any reaction from showing. The man was lying to protect her.

The witch-woman frowned deeply, and the gaze of the shaman fell back on Shulu. She sensed his magic probe her, reaching out and touching her. She hid her own magic, and allowed just a flutter of it to show. She seemed just as any witch-woman, at least to his senses. He thought the intruder was someone of about his strength, and that he could detect them. He was wrong.

Shulu, even now in her dotage, knew she was far stronger than he. She showed him what she wanted him to see, and he was fooled.

"Enough of this," he said with displeasure to the witch-woman. "Do not trouble me with your allegations again unless you have proof. Take that as a warning." He glared at her, and then strode out of the room.

The witch-woman cast a glance full of malice at Shulu, and stomped after her master.

"That woman has no love for you," the warrior on the bed said.

Shulu turned her attention to him. The witch-woman was nothing.

"You lied for me. Why?"

"Because I remember what she said. Even in my darkness her words reached me. But you…" he paused. "You, I remember for what you did."

"You should not remember."

"I do though. But have no fear of me. I am one who loves you for what you have done, and no word will ever escape my lips. Your secret is safe. At least, my lips will never unlock it. My loyalty is with you, today and forever."

Shulu felt her old heart begin to melt. For too long she had been exposed to all the terrible things in the world. But here was a good and simple man, and his untroubled loyalty to her was as a balm to her soul. There were people worth fighting for, and she would not forget.

"Rest, young warrior. Sleep, and know that Shulu Gan, Dragon of the Empire, thinks of you."

She left then, and went out into the training ground. The warriors there had commenced their training, and soon she was undertaking her work, healing slight injuries and offering advice to prevent them in future.

She made no fuss, and acted as any witch-woman would, but despite escaping detection this morning, she knew suspicion lay heavily on her. She must proceed with extreme caution now, for the slightest mistake would see her attacked, captured or killed.

And yet the risks she had recently taken had rewarded her. She knew more now of the enemy's plans than she had for some time, and she began to lay her own.

18. The Feast of Ravens

Shar felt a slow sense of joy building, and her gratitude to the cosmos was immense. Call it fate, luck, chance, or merely a random event, Asana recovered quickly from his injury.

They had spent several days in the cave, and each morning the local populace arrived with food and well wishes. Now, they were on the road again.

Asana sat upon a pony. It was not a young animal, but it was good-natured and sure-footed on the mountain trails. Shar had paid for this, though the locals had tried to refuse accepting any coin for it. She knew that these people, though not living in poverty, could ill afford such a gift for free.

It felt good to give back to the people, and to redistribute some of the wealth the shamans had stolen in the first place. And as Asana was recovering quickly, likely they would give the pony to a village before they started to descend into the lowlands.

Thinking of that brought a frown to Shar's face. She flicked her hair away from her eyes, and considered what the future might hold.

She did not know. She had no way of knowing. That the Skultic people were mobilizing for war was a given. They would certainly join up with her army down on the lowlands. But what then?

If things went according to plan, she would press eastward against the Nagrak border, but only a fool assumed plans would come to fruition exactly as they were laid.

The shamans would have their own plans. What were they?

If only she could put herself in the shoes of the enemy, to walk as they walked, see as they saw and think as they thought, then she might determine what action they would take.

They knew where she was. From that, if nothing else, they could calculate her intent. Raise an army to come against them from the opposite flank than they had prepared for. What action could they take to neutralize that? What action would she take in their place?

They would feel fear. The foundations of their world were being gnawed at, and far more successfully than they could ever have imagined. That would give them great motivation to strike out.

Would they seek to kill her? They were already trying that, but they could redouble their efforts. She must be wary. She was the head of the snake. Lop it off, and the body, though it might thrash for some time, would follow.

Chatchek was in greater danger too. If they could take it and destroy the threat from that flank, then what she was doing here, though still a risk to them, was something they would feel comfortable in handling. Chatchek was secure though. Nearly so secure as to be impregnable, but not quite. Magic was still a threat there, and they would risk any kind to meet there ends.

Or they could come against her here, in the far west of the Cheng lands. The Nagrak tribe was massive. They had the numbers to keep a siege going against Chatchek and still move against this new army forming against them. If so, the sooner they attacked the better. If they could destroy it before all its forces gathered, then the task would be so much easier.

But knowing and doing were not the same thing. It would take time for them to gather an army and march here.

She could not tell which of these tactics the enemy would try for. She must be ready for them all. That gave an urgency to her step though, for she did not like her new army gathering without her. Much as she trusted her generals, they did not have her experience.

The days passed slowly for her, and the marching never quick enough. Yet they covered much ground in the mountains, and that was no easy task. Many was the upward slope they climbed, the frozen brook they crossed, the forest they trod warily through, and the fields of snow they tramped over.

A time came when they found other warriors marching to the designated meeting place on the lowlands, and these they joined.

Their number swelled. They came close to the Nashwan Temple, but not within sight of it.

"I know where your heart lies, and what your sacred oath drives you to," Shar said to Asana one evening when the stars were bright and the temple less than a day away. If you choose to leave and seek out Bei-Mei, I will give you my blessing. He might yet live in, or near, the ruins of the temple."

She feared what answer he might give, but she was surprised.

"I will go with you, Nakatath. You're my friend, Shar, and you might need my help. This I would do in any case, but my heart tells me Bai-Mai is here no longer anyway. The temple is destroyed. He has sought to gain a following in Skultic, but that has certainly been rebuffed. He will join with his true loyalty now. The shamans. So my quickest way to bring justice to him is to stay with you."

Shar was relieved. She needed him, but she would not have kept him at her side against his will. Even if she could have.

The next day they descended the mountains and headed north. On the road, they caught up with more of their army.

It was a sizable force now. More would be ahead though, in fact the greater proportion by far. It gave Shar confidence though. If just the tail end was this large, then her efforts, or more properly Asana's efforts, had been worthwhile.

They came down the mountains into colder weather below. Or at least it seemed that way. A drizzle of rain fell, at times turning to sleet. But then a wind pushed through, blowing the clouds and rain away. It too was unpleasant, and for no small reason did the tribes avoid conflict during the winter months. This was proof of why.

The times were changing though. This was no longer the skirmishing of tribe against tribe. It was war. And doubtless the shamans would have taken cues from her. If she had hastened in the past and used speed of travel as a weapon, they would adopt the tactic. If she moved troops during winter, and even fought, so would they.

For all the unpleasantness of the weather, Shar forged on. Again and again they gathered bands of warriors to them that they caught up to on the road. They were an army now, and so far as Shar could calculate near half the size of the force that would have been mustered from Skultic.

Huigar, it seemed, had worked out what she was thinking.

"Not long now, Shar. Soon, we'll meet up with the army in Nahlim Forest, and then even the Nagrak hordes will be fearful. We'll have an army that can wreak havoc upon them."

124

"That's the plan," Shar agreed.

Asana, now walking and showing no sign of his terrible injury, agreed.

"When word reaches Kubodin that you've succeeded here, he'll break the siege at Chatchek and attack. The Nagraks will surely weaken their forces there to bolster the new one they must muster here."

That was what Shar hoped. But hoping was in vain. Only reality counted, and how one was able to transform dreams into truth.

They overtook another force before dusk. By dawn, they were on the march again. Shar ensured they worked together as a single unit, and she trained them as they went to respond to certain signals by horn and by flag. The same that the rest of her armies used. If ever they came together as one force, it would make them more effective.

By mid-morning, there were worrying signs.

"The ravens gather," Radatan said ominously.

He was right. Shar marched ahead at a faster pace, but she was sure to deploy extra scouts. The land about them was now open, flat and clear, so there did not appear to be any chance of ambush. But she was not taking any chances.

The ravens were thick in the sky, and so too were hawks and kites. As they got closer, no one was in any doubt that a battle had occurred.

Soon they saw it. Bodies lay sprawled over the ground, all still. But among them flapped the wings of carrion birds. Foxes and wild dogs were there too. They moved, fighting, snarling, flapping wings, jostling among each other over their grisly feast.

"It's sickening," Huigar muttered.

She was right, and Shar knew it. She knew also that she must go through that field and determine what had happened. Who had fought whom? Who had won? What did it mean for her army?

Most of her soldiers did not need to see it though. Not up close. Nothing sapped the morale of warriors more than seeing the end result of a battle they had not fought and survived themselves.

She picked a small band, including Radatan as the best tracker among them. They headed toward the remnants of the battle. The army she sent to skirt around the field. They would meet it on the other side.

"It's a day old," Radatan said.

The bodies had not begun to bloat yet, and neither was there a great stench. Shar guessed his assessment to be correct.

She stepped over a dead man, his sword still gripped in his hand, a wound in his side from which his intestines spilled to the ground. Something had torn at them, pulling them farther out. She could not tell if it had been a fox or a dog.

Suddenly a flash caught her eye near another body. Her hand reached for a sword, but it was only a raven. Boldgrim flicked his staff at it, but it did not fly away. Instead, it cocked a beady eye on him, its beak red with gore.

It was the same all over the battlefield. Foxes, dogs and carrion birds were everywhere, and they feasted. They paid little heed to the small group of living that walked among the dead.

"Here a shield wall stood against a cavalry attack," Radatan said, ignoring what was going on around him and merely doing his job of working out what had happened. "The wall buckled, and the defenders were cut down by light and curved blades."

Shar studied the wounds, and saw that he was right. There was a dead horse nearby, a long spear still protruding from its belly. A rider lay trapped beneath it where it fell, his hands still reaching out in death as they had when he breathed his last, trying to escape the weight that crushed him. She doubted he died quickly.

There were few dead horses. The attackers had won convincingly. Perhaps the defenders were unprepared, but more likely they were just badly outnumbered.

"The rider was a Nagrak," Asana said.

She had thought as much herself. It was her mistake. She should have ordered the army to gather in Skultic rather than stretching itself out in smaller groups to meet her other army from Nahlim Forest. It was her fault, and the death around her was horrific.

"You could not have guessed the Nagraks would act so quickly," Asana said gently.

Always he seemed to know what she was thinking. And he was right, but it did not help. It was still her fault.

"Over here," Radatan called out.

The Two Ravens warrior led them through the rows of corpses that lay there like a grisly forest that had been felled.

"See how the bodies lie more thickly?"

He was right. The corpses were numerous here, almost piled one atop another. There were more dead horses too. Perhaps they were more properly termed ponies. They were larger than the mounts Shar had seen Nagraks ride in the past, but no doubt in different areas of their vast tribal lands they kept different breeds.

They moved on for another hundred yards or so, and the dead bodies grew thicker. Shar saw a raven jerk back its head and try to swallow something. With disgust, she realized it was an eyeball. Again and again, it threw its head back, and anger welled in her.

She drew a sword and swung it, merely intended to scare the creature away. But fire flashed from the sword.

It wrapped around the raven, and it exploded in a puff of crimson fire.

She was stunned. That had never happened before. The power in the swords was growing stronger, as Shulu had warned her it would. *Blood feeds them.*

She could hear her grandmother's voice from one of their many lessons in childhood. *Blood feeds them. They are a two-edged weapon, Shar Fei. Remember.*

No one said anything. Boldgrim studied her speculatively though. The others looked everywhere but at her.

They went on. The defenders lay heaped now where they fell protecting their last leader.

"All their wounds are to the front. None behind," Radatan said.

Shar understood him. The hill tribes were a reserved people. They understood courage though, and valued it. These warriors had died fighting, and they had not turned and tried to flee.

"There lies the leader," Asana said.

He was a taller man, or he would have been in life. His head was hacked off, and through his body were many spear wounds and sword thrusts. They had struck him even after his death.

The head lay to the side, blankly staring at the sky. He had been an older man, at least compared to the warriors around him. Probably many were his relations.

"His name was Hropthar," one of the monks said quietly. "He came every second year to Nashwan Temple with goods to trade. We liked him."

Radatan looked around. "They were not taken by surprise. The Nagraks came at them from the east, and in great number. Their force was four or five times stronger, mostly mounted. A good defense was made, but to no avail." The hunter paused. "But there are other tracks, hard to see because of the battle. They are older. The dead around us were not the first of the Skultic warriors to come this way. There is an army still ahead of us, assuming the Nagraks haven't attacked them already."

Shar knew what to do instantly. Or at least what she would do. She owed the warriors who flocked to her banner every protection she could offer.

"Then we shall catch up to them as fast as may be, and share their fate, whatever it is."

They hastened through the army of the dead then, and the foxes and dogs gave ground grudgingly while the ravens and kites fluttered briefly into the air before settling down again after they passed.

Shar could not save the dead. But the living, for them she would do all she could. The swords burned against her thighs as she strode forward, and her violet eyes flashed.

"We march to battle!" Shar said when she came up to the bulk of her force. "The enemy has inflicted damage on us. Will we take that? Or will we hit them back?"

"Hit them back!" came the reply. And it was heartfelt. The dead were of their tribe, in some cases of their kin.

The scouts came and went. Radatan chief among them. They moved forward rapidly during the day. Stopped for a meal at dusk and half a night's sleep, then pressed forward in the dark.

"A dangerous tactic," Boldgrim said.

"I'm in a dangerous mood," Shar replied.

He eyed her again, as he had done before. Quite what he could make of her, she was not sure. She trusted him though. She hoped he felt the same about her.

Dawn came. The day was bright, if cold. They stopped for a rest and breakfast, and scouts returned with news.

Another battle was ahead of them. Perhaps only an hour away, but the two forces were maneuvering, and though battle had been joined several times it had also broken off. The two forces were more evenly matched than in the battle behind them.

Shar gave a signal. A horn was blown, and the army hastened forward, quiet but eager.

19. To the Last Breath

The scouts had judged the matter correctly. Within an hour, Shar's army approached the forces ahead of them.

There had already been skirmishes in different places. Likely enough, the full army of the enemy had not approached the warriors of Skultic at that point. It had merely been an advanced force, yet one sufficiently large to instigate combat.

Whomsoever commanded the Skultic forces had wanted no part of that. Shar liked him. He had withdrawn, sought more favorable ground, and maneuvered several times so as to delay a decisive battle.

"He knows we are coming," Boldgrim said.

Shar narrowed her eyes. For all that he was a shaman, he had grasped the military situation much faster than any shaman would be expected to. But then again, he was of a different ilk than these later day sorcerers. He came of a time when battle and strife had marched across the land. Now, the shamans grew fat and lazy on the hard work of their subjects.

"Us, or perhaps just more Skultic forces," she replied. "He may not know the fate of those men we saw yesterday."

"He is trying to come toward us now," Asana said quietly.

Shar shaded her eyes with her hand and tried to see over the great distance. It was true. He was certainly moving, but the enemy force was coming in from the east and would engage with him before he had a chance. Even farther away was a cloud of dust. It was the only visible sign of the larger force of Nagraks that the scouts had warned her of.

Shar arranged her army. It was tired, and yet the enemy could not have expected them to be here so quickly. No doubt their own scouts were in the field too.

She had no cavalry. All she could do was form in a square, and she chose the front ranks as spearmen.

"Forward!" she commanded.

The square moved. It did not hold perfect formation, for they were yet ill-trained.

"Trot!" Shar commanded, and the signal was sent through her force. It moved forward briskly.

They would not be in time to help the other force from Skultic. Not if it were defeated in the first attack that was coming against it. That looked to be soon. But if it could hold its own, she would be there presently.

In the distance, the far army was now visible, even if only as flashes of light from metal beneath the cloud of dust. That gave her pause for thought. She did not know how large it was, for reports varied and information from the scouts was scarce. But to raise dust in winter meant it was large indeed. There was no snow here. The grass was sere from frost, but it had rained not long ago. The earth had not dried out greatly even if the grass was withered.

It gave her pause for thought. This was a fight she might not win. She could back out now, but if she did so her allies would die. Not only that, it would strike hard at morale. Who would want to fight for her if she were not willing to fight for them?

She pressed ahead, although she saw the looks of several of her friends. They knew, and they understood.

Ahead the Skultic force and the oncoming Nagraks finally clashed. Dimly the sound of battle traveled over the grassland. There were screams and shouts. Men died, but the Nagrak riders mostly veered away at the last moment. The shield wall defeated them.

The Nagraks wheeled around. It seemed to Shar they hurried, for they knew this was the best chance of defeating their opponent. Shortly, the force they were trying to destroy would outnumber them. But not when their own reinforcements arrived. This, however, they did not intend to wait for. The commander wanted victory for himself.

Again the riders bore down on the shield wall. Curved swords glinted in the sun. The thunder of their approach was a slow rumble drifting over the grassland. Slow, but giving the impression of great power.

The shield wall buckled even before the riders made contact. Shar understood immediately. It was a ploy.

The first rank of the shield wall merely withdrew, and behind them strode forward another line. These held long spears, and they knelt. The butts of the spears were anchored in the ground. The points raised up at an angle.

In confusion, the riders pulled their horses up. Not that the horses would continue into the wall anyway. But the spearmen sprang forward at that very moment, and they thrust their weapons. Many riders fell. They could not bring their much shorter range weapons to bear.

A horn sounded. Once more the Nagraks wheeled away. They left many dead behind them though. Nor did they attack again. They withdrew to a safe distance, and there they waited.

The Skultic force moved, maintaining its shape well. It came toward Shar. Shar sped toward it. When their groups were within shouting distance, greetings were exchanged. There were men on both sides who knew one another, and the hopes of those who had just fought were raised. This was no trap. This was their countrymen come to help them.

Shar ordered her force to continue the square of the one they joined, and the two front lines now became one, facing the enemy.

It was not long before the commander of the force they had hurried to help came to Shar to offer thanks.

He was an old man. His hair was long and silver, his weathered skin tanned deeply by the sun. He was missing a tooth, scars crisscrossed his forearms and one long one cut diagonally across his face.

Old the man might be, but his eyes were bright and his step firm.

"Hail, Shar Fei, emperor-to-be."

"You were in command of these men?"

"I was."

"Then you have my thanks. You did well under difficult circumstances. I'm impressed."

The old man bowed deeply.

"What is your name?" Shar asked.

"His name," Asana interrupted, "is Chun Wah."

The old man turned his glance to Asana. "I had heard you were in these parts again. It's good to see you. And I hear you are now abbot."

Asana shook the old man's hand. "I am. Master Kaan is dead, murdered by Bei-Mai."

"I had heard that too." There was steel in the old man's voice, and something personal there.

"You two have met before?" Shar asked.

"Chun Wah, once upon a time, was a monk. He has the skills and training of the Nashwan Temple. He will be of great help to you, Shar."

The other monks showed keen interest at this. It was obviously before their time, but he was one of them even if for some reason he had left the temple.

"I don't doubt it. For now, we'd better concentrate on the enemy. Battle will be joined again soon."

Even as she spoke the enemy force was being joined by the greater force that came up behind it.

"We are outnumbered," Asana said.

That was becoming increasingly clear. The enemy was twice, perhaps three times their own size.

"And they are mounted," Huigar observed.

Shar was considering that too. Her options were limited. Extremely limited. She could not evade the enemy. They could travel faster. But to fight them was to contend against a much greater force.

She was beaten. Except, perhaps, by some stroke of luck. One thing that was in her favor was the lack of enemy foot soldiers. As long as her shield walls held against a cavalry charge, which they would assuming the men held their nerve, there would be no real fighting. Horses would not charge into an obstacle. It was only if the men grew scared and retreated that the enemy could get among them and bring their swords to bear. That would be the end.

"Are the Nagraks likely to dismount if their cavalry charges fail?"

"It's not their way," Asana answered her.

That was what she thought, too. It was good to hear it from Asana though. Of them all, he was the most widely traveled and experienced. Still, it was no certainty. Much depended on the enemy commander. Would he be willing to try something new to his tribe? Would the warriors of his tribe obey him?

"Here they come," Boldgrim said.

Shar watched in silence. She cultivated a look of calm. She knew many eyes were on her, and if she showed indications of anxiety it would ripple through the army.

A mass of the enemy approached. The hooves of their ponies was as thunder. Their curved swords flashed, and battle cries filled the air. This was mostly drowned out by the trampling hooves.

From the defenders an answering cry went up. So too did their spears in a prickly barrier. The horses hurtled toward it.

The men had courage. It was difficult to stay still and hold formation when a mass of horses charged. But they did so. They had learned from their previous success.

It was the horses that balked. Though their riders urged them on, the animals saw the barrier and wheeled to the side. Again this was a killing opportunity, and what archers there were and spear throwers took a toll upon the enemy.

The Nagraks raced away, and the Skultic warriors jeered them.

Shar was pleased. So far so good, but this was still a losing battle, even if the enemy would not win it quickly. How long before their commander changed tactics?

He did so quickly, but not, Shar thought, to any great advantage.

The Nagraks divided, and they raced around so that all four sides of the Skultic square was surrounded. She had anticipated this, and spearmen were on all four flanks. So too had they been given critical advice. *Hold your position. The horses will turn away. If you break formation, you will die.*

It was good advice. The proof of it had just played out, but soon new warriors would be tested. It was one thing to see. It was another to *do*.

The enemy commander was hardly innovative or daring, but he was swift. All at once a signal was given and again the enemy cavalry hurtled forward.

"He's not a quick learner," Radatan said.

"He has numbers to play with though," Boldgrim replied.

The charge came on. The Nagraks made as much noise as they could, trying to intimidate the defenders.

Yet all the four flanks held, though the north flank not as well as the others.

The Nagraks withdrew. They had failed, but Shar guessed what was coming next.

"He'll try the same thing again, only with more riders coming against our north. I think, perhaps, I'll let myself be seen there."

"That's dangerous," Huigar said.

"Not doing it is more dangerous still."

She hurried through the ranks of her own force. Her comrades came with her, and all about them were surprised greetings.

"Shar Fei!" some said. "Nakatath!" others called out. "Emperor!" still others yelled. She wished that last was true, but it looked near hopeless now.

As she walked she drew her swords, and she let the light of battle blaze in her violet eyes. She was a kind of legend to these warriors, many of whom had never seen her. The army stirred. She felt its heartbeat liven with spirit, and only just in time came to the north flank.

It was no surprise to see Chun Wah there. He would have read the situation the same as she.

"Not long now," he said.

Even as he spoke she came to the front rank and saw the Nagrak riders on this side begin to trot toward them. The enemy commander had doubled their number. It was, perhaps, too many. They would get in one another's way, but the sight of that many riders coming at an army was bound to instill fear.

The defenders set themselves though. The riders came on, gathering momentum. They cried out, making as much noise as they could to go with the deafening rumble of hooves.

Shar called out, lifting her twin swords high. "For Skultic! For the Cheng people! For a free life!"

137

This was not an army that knew her well, or she it. What her words would do, she could not be sure.

The riders hurtled in. Yet again though, they wheeled at the last moment. The spear wall of the Skultic force held firm, firmer than the previous charge.

Missiles were hurled. Spears, arrows and even rocks. Enemy riders fell and horses went down. The charge had failed, and the cavalry turned and fled in ignominy.

"They'll come against us on foot now," Chun Wah said. There was no emotion in his voice. He might as well have been talking about the weather, but they both knew what it meant.

The swords of the Nagraks were curved, and better suited to slashing from horseback. It was their preferred method of fighting. Yet it had failed. The enemy commander could not allow that to stand. He would be answerable to the shamans, and he would not want to tell them that his far superior force had been beaten. On foot they would come, whether the Nagraks liked to fight that way or not. And even if they were unused to it, by doing so they could start an actual battle.

It was one they would win. They had the greater force, and their numbers would tell.

So it proved. The enemy advanced on foot, and if they did so grudgingly, they still yelled war cries and came on with enthusiasm. Or were driven hard from behind.

The forces clashed. There was no wheeling away this time. There was no skirmish. This was a drawn out battle to the death. And warriors died on both sides.

The enemy came at them from four directions. The Skultic force held its own. They had won the skirmishes before. They were better used to fighting on foot, and they held close ranks and stabbed forward with their swords while the enemy tried to slash with their curved swords.

138

If the numbers were even, the Skultic force would win. But they were not, and the enemy could afford the greater losses they were sustaining.

Worse, the enemy warriors came for Shar. If they killed her, the battle was over, and they knew it.

20. Words in the Dark

Tiredness swamped Kubodin. It was a weakness that stole all from him, and though the sky grayed in the east he was not sure he would see the dawn.

Somehow, he kept going. He could not have done so without help.

"Not far now," the captain said.

Kubodin owed that man a lot. He would promote him, if he lived. Twice he fainted on his feet, and came to still standing, supported by his helpers.

Finally, they were at the barracks where the Nahat kept to themselves. Those not on the wall. The captain banged loudly at the door and it was opened swiftly. One look the Nahat gave Kubodin, and then gestured sharply to bring him inside.

Again, Kubodin nearly fell, and he saw a trail of blood on the floor behind him when he was eased down into a bunk bed.

They gathered around him. He tried to speak, but he was hushed. His tunic was removed, and so too the bandages. The wound was cleaned and cauterized, and that brought him out of his stupor. It hurt. But pain was good. Pain meant he was still alive.

Then the stitching began. That hurt as well, but for this they gave him a tea to drink, and that dulled the pain quickly. Or it might have been some concoction they put on the wound, for he saw they used dry herbs and some kind of paste out of an earthenware jar. No doubt it would help fight infection too.

He had made the right choice. If anyone could save him, it was these men.

The room began to swim as though he were drunk.

"Rest," came a voice. He was not sure which Nahat spoke. He did not know all their names, but each would be a friend to him for life now.

"Let no one know," he muttered, and then darkness swallowed his mind.

He dreamed of his childhood. And in the forests of the Wahlum Hills men stepped out from the shadowy trees, swords and knives drawn to kill him. Again and again he dreamed, and each dream was worse than the last. At length though he slipped into oblivion and found rest.

He woke. Bright light streamed in from the windows, and the barracks were warm. One of the Nahat sat near him, leaning forward in his chair.

"What time is it?" Kubodin asked.

"Mid-afternoon. You have slept a long time, and just as well. You needed it."

"I take it I'll live?"

"You're a strong man. But the wound was dangerous, and you lost much blood."

Kubodin noted the reply. It actually did not answer his question, so the wound really was as bad as he thought, and he was not quite safe yet. Otherwise the shaman would not have evaded a direct response. Nevertheless, he felt that a little of his strength had returned.

"Have the Nagraks done anything?"

"No. All is well on the battlement."

"Is there any other news?"

"Some. There is a rumor flying throughout the whole compound."

"What rumor is that?"

"That you are dead. Assassinated. That Shar's army is leaderless, and the chiefs cannot decide who is best to take your place."

"Do the chiefs believe it?" That was what was critical at the moment. If they began to fight among themselves, the defense might fall apart.

"We have told them nothing. That was your order. For the moment, they are confused. They are seeking you everywhere to discover the truth."

That was an understandable reaction. And a good one. The rumors would be what they were. He could not expect so many people to see him as he was last night, and for all of them to stay silent. It only took one to speak, even in confidence, and word would spread. When it did, it would change and twist as well. That was the nature of gossip.

"There is another rumor too," the Nahat said.

Kubodin already felt that he had begun to tax what was left of his strength, but he needed to find out what was happening and take what steps he could.

"Out with it, then," he replied.

"The rumor holds that we are betrayed from within. That enemies walk in our midst."

"And what do you think?"

The Nahat paused. "I have seen your wounds. The enemy is among us."

Kubodin hesitated. All he could do here was tell the truth, but what was *that*? He was not sure himself.

"Shar's army has been infiltrated. We always knew it would be. To what extent, I don't know. There were only a handful of men last night that tried to kill me, and most of those are dead. Are there more? Probably. But I think not many. Otherwise, they would have tried something before now."

"However few, they will certainly try again."

"I'll be on better guard from now on. They tricked me last night, and I was very lucky. They'll not get a second chance."

The Nahat did not look convinced. Not on any of those issues, but skepticism was a good trait, and Kubodin was not convinced himself. What mattered was not the things he did not know and could not control, but the actions he could take.

"I have to get out and about, and be seen by the soldiers. That's the only way to calm things down, and to deprive the enemy of any advantage."

"Out of the question," the Nahat said. "Maybe in two days' time. You were on the brink of death last night, and things might still go badly if you get an infection."

Kubodin thought hard. The man was right. But being right did not matter. More was needed right now, and only being seen on the battlement, in front of friend and foe alike, would achieve it.

"You're right. But the army needs me now. I'll compromise though. I'll rest until late this afternoon. Then I'll go, be seen, and come straight back here."

The Nahat was not impressed, but he did not argue either.

"It may kill you. So long as you know that. I'll let Ravengrim know, and he'll go with you."

The reason was unspoken. The enemy had tried to kill him, and they would try again. The best time for that was while he was weak. He needed protection.

It was not a long period of rest ahead of him, but Kubodin turned his head into the pillow and slept almost instantly. Sleep was often the best medicine to counteract illness, and the best cure for injury. If enough could be had.

It did not seem long before he woke. Straightaway he knew by the light coming in from the window that it was already late afternoon, and he had best hurry.

"Are you sure you want to go ahead with this foolishness?"

It was Ravengrim. Perhaps there was rebuke in his tone for the fact that Kubodin had not asked him along when he had been tricked into going to the well. Or perhaps it was just a statement of fact, as he saw it.

"You know as well as I that I must go. I have to be seen by the soldiers. And I must be seen by the chiefs, or the generals as they're more properly called now."

All he got from Ravengrim was a grunt. It was as close as he was going to get to a yes. Quickly, he dressed, and he hid his dizziness and weakness.

No one seemed to notice. It was a good sign because he must do the same before Shar's army.

When he was ready, he looked Ravengrim squarely in the eye.

"You know why I have to do this."

"I understand the need for it. Whether you are up to it is another matter. If you reopen your wound, you might die."

They left the barracks then, just the two of them. It would look more normal that way, and if they were attacked Ravengrim, old as he was, did not lack the ability to defend himself. And Kubodin had his axe.

He noticed the axe was clean. The Nahat had tended to it while he slept, and he felt a pang of anger at that. They had no right to touch it. But the anger drifted away. It was unfounded, and they had not stolen it or anything of that kind. Still, he held the haft as he walked.

The stairs going up the battlement nearly defeated him. He took them slowly, and tried to hide his shortness of breath and the pain that flared in his wounds.

As he walked, soldiers greeted him. He saw the surprise on their faces, and the relief, and that told him all he needed to know. His decision had been right.

By the time he reached the battlements the men were cheering. Among them were some chiefs. He should have told them the truth, and he would. There had been no time though.

He walked some distance along the rampart, but chose not to go too far. Already he was short of breath, and the pain of his wounds was returning.

Even so, he did not even grimace. Somewhere, perhaps close, was one of those who had attacked him. If not, then someone who was part of their group and would inform them. And from them back to the enemy shamans. He would show no weakness. He would show that they had failed. He would dishearten them.

All eyes were on him, and he spoke. "You've heard rumors," he said. "As you can see, I'm well. Dead? Not me! Not this day. I'll live to spit in the eye of the enemy and insult them as they run away in fear!"

The men liked that. They clapped and hollered.

"I am here," he said. "I am strong! Let not words in the dark undo what our swords have won!"

They cheered at that, and he gave them a jaunty wave and signaled to Ravengrim to start returning to the barracks.

"Get me out of here," he whispered. "If I stumble, give me no more help than you must."

Somehow, he made it along the rampart, waving as he went and jesting with the men. When he came to the stairs, he nearly fell, but a deft touch from Ravengrim at his elbow was enough for him to keep his balance.

He was not sure how, but he got back to the barracks. As soon as he was out of sight of any but the Nahat though, he collapsed.

145

Blood welled from his injury.

21. A Voice in the Dark

Kubodin was surrounded by a great dark, and in his dreams, he felt it hunger for him.

The pain of his wound was there. He felt it ache. So too he sensed his weakness through delirium. If delirium it was, for he saw many things and they seemed real. He was conscious enough to be aware of where his body lay and that he had taxed himself beyond endurance. He was dreaming, but it was a wakeful dream such as he had heard legends tell of.

Dark legends. Stories of shamans and their magic. Stories where they journeyed as spirits.

You are close to death, a voice spoke to him from out of the dark.

Kubodin wheeled around. There was no one there. He was in a forest. Not just any forest, but in Two Ravens' country. He would know his homeland anywhere, waking or sleeping. It was in his blood.

Death stalks you, old friend. Failure is with him. Defeat is by his side. For when you die, Shar's army will wither also.

Again, Kubodin spun around. He saw nothing but the shadowy trees. He noticed though that it was night, but no stars showed in the deadened sky. It was void of everything, including clouds. Not even a bat winged through it.

"Who are you that speaks from the forest, but cannot be seen?"

You know who I am. And you know I speak truth.

Truth, in Kubodin's experience, was a slippery fish. Just when you thought you had it the thing flicked its tail and splashed away.

He thought of the army though. Would it fall apart without him? Probably it would. Shar had given him command, and the warriors and chiefs accepted it because it was her choice. And she was Nakatath. But if he died, there was no clear succession. The chiefs would bicker among themselves. The warriors would see this, and the tribal nature of the Cheng empire would come to the fore again. The shamans would win. A thousand years of thinking was hard to put aside. Only Shar had the power to enforce her will. Maybe Asana could take her place. Both of those were apart from the tribes. They were separate. But he was a Two Raven man.

Then again, he who sought to predict the future was too stupid to realize he was not wise. One of the chiefs might rise into something more than they were now. The moment made the man, not the man the moment.

"Maybe," he said aloud. "Maybe not. You know nothing more than I do."

Perhaps I do. My memory stretches back to the beginning of time. Allow me the wisdom that is my due, and heed me.

"I know who you are. You are the demon in my axe, and I give you respect. As I give a weapon respect. But I don't let a blade do my thinking for me. Or ever would I be at war."

Wise words. And have I ever failed you? Now heed me. I seek not to command. You know I cannot. Not entrapped in this metal prison of Shulu Gan's crafting. I seek to guide you by wisdom, and leave the choice to you.

"Speak on, then."

I have this only to say. You are needed. You know that. Your enemy knows that. Otherwise, they would not have tried to kill you, as yet they still do. But I, and I alone, can make you strong. Strong

148

as Chatchek Fortress. Strong to withstand your enemies. Strong to endure in your physical body, which is weak. One sword thrust, one drop of poison in your food, and you die. I can guard you against such mischances. Magic can fortify you.

Kubodin felt temptation. He also knew that to give in was but the first step of several, and in the end his soul would be forfeit. But for Shar, and the Cheng Empire, might it not be worth it?

Kubodin closed his eyes. The forest disappeared, but he still sensed a presence all around him.

"No, demon. I'll take my chances."

There was a moment's silence. The dark pressed in against him, but he relaxed into it. What would be would be. If he died, he had lived a good life. The world would get on without him.

As you wish, came the answer. There was no chagrin in it, which was a surprise. But it was said demons had great patience.

The world seemed to fall away. Kubodin felt dizzy, and his stomach rose toward his throat like it did when he jumped from a height.

He woke, and felt the sheets beneath him. They were wet with sweat. Several of the Nahat were around him, their expressions concerned. In his hand was the axe, and his arm cramped because of the tightness of his grip.

"Let it go," one of the Nahat said.

Kubodin tried. But his hand was locked in place.

He used the other hand to pry free his grip, and at last the axe fell to the bed and his hand came free.

"That axe will kill you," one of the Nahat said.

"It can get in line for the chance with shamans, enemy soldiers and assassins," Kubodin replied.

"No. That axe is more dangerous than all else," Ravengrim said. "Be wary. I know what is in it. All the shamans in the world, standing together, would fear it."

It was a sobering thought, but Ravengrim was not done.

"Know this, general and chief. While you slept, tossing and turning, you held tight the axe. We feared you might injure yourself with it, or one who tended you. But try as we might, we could not prise it from your hand."

That was worse. Even so, he did not fear the axe. No harm had come to anyone, and he was in control. He would *always* be in control. Something disturbed him, but it was time to let it go. More important matters needed dealing with, and he felt strong, stronger than he had in a long time.

"And my wound?" he asked.

"Stitched again," Ravengrim told him. "And there is no infection, and despite your ill-advised jaunt along the battlements, you seem to be healing very fast. Faster than I have ever seen."

Ravengrim rarely showed anything of what he thought, but he had allowed a tone to creep into his voice. It might have been skepticism, or doubt. But of what, he chose not to say.

He rested for the remainder of the night, but he had given orders that his whereabouts could now be revealed to the chiefs. By morning, he had received various visits, caught up on what was happening and started to receive regular reports.

In truth, there was nothing to report. Not anything of consequence. The enemy had not attacked again, and morale among the defenders remained high.

The little news there was concerned basic operations of the enemy. They were preparing for winter, and part of that involved felling trees from the nearby woods. With these, they began to build makeshift shelters.

Kubodin did not envy them. Before winter was done, they would be burning them as fuel to stay warm. There were not enough trees nearby from which to both build shelters and to supply firewood for warmth and cooking.

The problems of the enemy were his problems too, in a strange way. A desperate enemy resorted to desperate tactics. Winter was only just starting. Already they would have problems, but as time progressed those problems would worsen.

Sickness would strike them. Winter was a time of year for illness. Add to it the proximity of the troops, and the sicknesses would spread rapidly. Food, or the lack of it, would play a role too. An encamped army in winter had a poor supply of nutrients, especially from fruit and vegetables. Malnutrition would make them more vulnerable to illness.

And there was the cold. Withering, murderous cold. They must endure that out of doors, and if the army leadership kept makeshift shelters to protect themselves while the common warriors huddled together against the wind, then morale would plummet. It could lead to rebellion.

The enemy leadership knew all this. They would be trying hard to find a way to win before the deeps of winter. But what could they do? He did not know. That he could think of no suitable plan did not mean they would not. After all, they were desperate while he was not. It was a factor that changed thinking.

He had no answers, but he knew they would try something. No doubt they would continue to try to kill him. And perhaps assassinate others. *That* he could foresee and take steps against. It was the unknown that would see him undone if he were not careful.

Argash entered the barracks at that point. His face was deadly serious, and Kubodin knew it was bad news. He caught his eye though, and waved him over.

151

Argash approached. "We have a problem, Kubodin. A serious one."

22. Agents of Influence

Kubodin resisted the urge to sigh. Even more to say that he was tired of problems. Leadership was about setting an example.

"What has happened?"

"Several things," Argash replied, pulling up a chair and sitting by the bed. He did not ask what had happened to cause Kubodin an injury. He knew, and he knew also it was best that as little was said as possible. What he did not know, he could not repeat.

"They all stem from our enemies, and have but one purpose. First is this. Several fires have been lit, mostly at the outside of well-used barracks and those areas where food and equipment is stored."

That was bad news, but they had expected and planned for it.

"What damage was done?"

"Very little," Argash said. "Our patrols spotted them and put them out swiftly."

"Were any of the perpetrators caught?"

"No. But they were seen. It doesn't appear to be a large group, but there's no way to know if they keep themselves separate so as to evade capture all in one go."

Kubodin did not think there were many of them. But even one could cause a great deal of damage if he had luck.

"What else?"

"An attack was made on one of the wells. It was later in the night. We don't know if it was the same group or a different one."

"It was repelled?"

153

"Fairly easily. Two of the attackers were killed, and one defender."

Kubodin considered that. It reinforced the idea that there were not many traitors. Surely, they would have attacked with the greatest force they could muster. If it were not enough, that meant that more likely they were desperate rather than foolish or splitting their forces.

It did fit together. Their attempt on his own life had failed, and now they feared for their own. To fail the shamans was a risky business. There would be threats and ramifications. The shamans would not be so foolhardy as to actually kill any of the few servants they had in the fortress, but they would certainly threaten them. And if retribution could not be swift, the traitors might believe that eventually Shar would fail and the shamans would exact their revenge at a later date. And they would too. The shamans had long memories.

"Has anything else happened?"

Argash gave him a flicker of a smile. "Despite your appearance on the ramparts, there's a rumor that you're dead. It's growing. And the other rumor with it is that Shar is dead too, and that's why your luck failed. Her magic no longer protects you."

"Do I look dead?"

"No, but that's the rumor."

"It's preposterous."

"Even so, there are those who believe it. There are those who believe anything they're told, and they pass it on as though it were a truth."

That was certainly true. But it was not happening by accident.

"We have agents of influence in the compound, Argash. Probably someone separate from the warriors who attacked … me and the well."

"So you *were* attacked?"

"Of course. You worked that out already. It doesn't matter though. They failed, and they won't get another chance. Tell that to anyone who asks," he said.

What to do about this new development was not an easy task.

"The saboteurs," he said, "we've stymied. They can do damage. A lot if they're lucky. But they *do* need luck. Otherwise, they're only a nuisance."

"But the agents of influence," Argash perceived his thoughts, "are another matter."

"Exactly. How can we counter them? And for all that they only deal with words as weapons, in the end that might be more dangerous than anything."

Argash pursed his lips, and remained silent while he thought.

"All we can do is tell the truth. As you did on the battlements. Most people guessed that you had been attacked, but it didn't really matter so long as you survived it. You *showed* them you did. You gave them evidence they could see and believe. We must keep doing that."

"It won't always be so easy. For instance, how can we convince people that Shar yet lives?"

Argash had no answer for that, and he said so.

"Perhaps," Kubodin went on, "just proving the rumors wrong when they crop up is enough, and if we can't prove them *all* wrong, then the times we have exposed them in the past will give us credibility."

"I can't see what else we can do. There's no way to discover where the first whisper comes from before it grows into a rumor."

That was right, but Kubodin did not like it. If only they could discover such a thing, then they could stomp out the fire before it was lit. They could stifle that influence designed to undermine and sap morale before it had a chance to arise.

Then a thought occurred to him, and he saw Ravengrim talking to one of the Nahat, and beckoned him over.

"I have a question for you," Kubodin said.

"You should be sleeping," Ravengrim replied, and he gave Argash a meaningful look, which the chief pretended not to notice.

Kubodin explained the situation to him, and Ravengrim nodded absently.

"I see your point. This agent of influence, or this group of them, is more dangerous in a way than saboteurs. But what can the Nahat do about it?"

"Perhaps nothing," Kubodin said. "I don't know the ways of magic. And yet there might be something. I think there is."

"What?"

"I think there's communication going on between the shamans outside and their infiltrators in here. What's being done smells of a master plan, and of someone giving orders. Too much has happened too fast and in too much of a coordinated way."

Ravengrim frowned. "You could be right. It does feel that way."

"And if I am, how is the communication accomplished? The ramparts are guarded. No enemy can approach that way."

"Perhaps some kind of signal system at night with lights," Argash suggested.

"That may be," Kubodin agreed. "Designate men to look for such a thing. But I think something else is going on." He glanced at Ravengrim.

The Nahat had lost his absent-minded look. Now his eyes were fierce, and his gaze was like a hawk's.

"I know what you're suggesting. Magic."

156

"Exactly. Are there not ways to convey messages by magic, even to someone who isn't a shaman. And if that's what they're doing, can you detect it and find out where the spies are?"

23. Oneness

Ravengrim was in doubt.

It was not a mood that he liked. Nor one that he had often felt. However, the chief had given him a task. No, the *general* had given him a task. Shar Fei, like her great ancestor, had raised a mighty army and held it together. She had unified the scattered tribes. At least in part. What was happening now had happened a thousand years ago, and it was a title of greater respect to be called general in an age such as this than to be named chief.

Was the task possible though? Could magic be used to detect magic? Certainly. Could it be used to trace such subtle magic as might be used in communication between the shamans outside the wall and the agents of influence within? That had never been done before. Not that he knew of.

It did not matter. He must find a way, for he saw as well as Kubodin that words were a dangerous enemy at the moment. Swords were sheathed, but the war was still being fought. A deadly blow could be struck without ever a weapon being lifted.

He knew what was required to find the answers he needed. His was but one mind. Instead, he needed the minds of all the Nahat. They must commune.

Many of his brothers were on the wall. Some were in the barracks. It was of no matter.

He sent his mind out of his body, feeling it float free of the shackles of the flesh.

"Brothers," he called into the dreamworld that overlaid reality.

"I attend," came the answers from his brethren, wherever they were. With their voices came a shadow-form of them, floating in the dreamworld and gathering around his own.

He sat by one of the many hearths in the barracks. A fire burned behind him. Shar had great foresight, and ensured masses of firewood were brought into the fortress, both as a means of warmth and cooking, but also to give a sense of superiority over the enemy. The one was indoors in comfort, while the other struggled in the outdoors. It was a stimulus for morale. All the more so if the enemy ran out of firewood toward the end of winter, which she anticipated would happen through bad planning. The shamans had not been trained as she in the logistics of war.

Before him stood the shadow-forms of all the Nahat, and his own shadow-form stood before his body in the chair. To all others but the Nahat, it would appear that he sat there by himself, a distracted look on his face. That was all.

He spoke of his conversation with Kubodin, and told them the task that had been set.

"Can it be done?" he finished.

"The point of the general is well made. If the communication is by magic, why should we not be able to detect it if we try hard?" said one.

"We don't know that magic is being used," said another. "It is only a guess."

"A good guess though," replied Ravengrim. To this, most nodded agreement.

"A good guess," said one of the brothers. "Yet not so easy to detect, I think. The magic is slight. Very slight. Unless by chance we stood close to someone being spoken to, I don't think we can sense it. That is too unlikely."

That was true, and Ravengrim had considered it. One idea led to another though.

"Yet it remains probable that they communicate from without to within, and there is likely no shaman within. So how is it done? From mind to mind as we commune now? I think not. They must have an artifact to give them the magic they do not possess naturally. One made by the shamans for such a purpose. Of old, there were items that did this."

It was sound reasoning, and though no words were spoken he sensed the mood of the Nahat. They were in agreement, and he felt the undercurrent of emotion that went with that, hard to read in real life, and yet in the dreamworld much stronger.

"We are convinced," came the answer after a pause. It was as one voice, but all the Nahat were in it.

Runeguard spoke then. "Even so, how does this help us? An artifact would be more easy to detect, especially while in use, but the magic is still small. It is nothing more than a touch of minds. Our chances of discovering the agents of influence rise if you are right, but they are still slim."

That was correct. A thought had been growing in Ravengrim though, and now it blossomed.

"There is a way. The more I think of it, the more I believe we must attempt it. Not just to fulfil this necessary task, but to grow our knowledge of magic."

He sensed their unease at that answer. No. Unease was not quite right. Uncertainty blended with anticipation.

"What way?" one asked. It did not matter who. He spoke for them all.

"I speak of the sorcery known as *oneness*. Was not such magic used in the Shadowed Wars? Can we not join as we commune now, but more strongly? Can we not together form a being of one body, one mind and one spirit? The

160

stories say it is possible. And such a single being comprised of us all has great power. It could sense what we as individuals cannot. It could detect the artifact."

Ravengrim sensed their shock. It was not something they had anticipated. He perceived fear and wariness. He recognized doubt too, as well there should be, for long ages had passed in the world since this sorcery had been attempted.

Most of all though, he felt the growing idea of knowledge. They could learn from this. It was a chance to transform their art, and magic *was* an art. It thrived on taking risks. It was a science too, and science likewise thrived on experimentation.

They could not resist. He felt the overwhelming emotion of acceptance before one of them spoke.

"We will do it. There are dangers. Perhaps the risk is even greater than we know. It has not been done in so long that the knowledge of it is forgotten. Yet we must gather that knowledge back and rescue it before it slides completely into oblivion."

There was another voice from out of the midst of the many.

"All this is so. Yet we have another task to fulfill. We must protect the fortress. If the sorcery is as dangerous as we think it may be, then there is the risk of death. If we all join in oneness, and perish, then the fortress is vulnerable to the enemy shamans."

It was a good thought, and Ravengrim acknowledged it.

"You are right, brother. I propose that fifteen of us join in oneness, and the remainder stay aloof. And safe. That way we can attempt to fulfill both our tasks, and not have one risk the other."

This they agreed on, and they decided to wait until nighttime, and the period between when dinner was finished and midnight was approaching, to try the experiment. It was during that window of time that the shamans were most like to attempt to communicate with their allies inside the fortress.

Night came over the fortress as any other. For the Nahat though, it was a special evening that beckoned in a new age. The sorcery they would attempt was ancient. Their enemy shamans may have tried it in the last thousand years, but it was unlikely. The dangers and uncertainty was high. And they had not been pressed by circumstances to take any risks. They ruled, and until now that had never seriously been challenged. What need had they to hazard themselves?

The age was turning though. The enemy *had* risked, and lost, in their dabbling into the demonic world. If the Nahat did not keep up, and try something themselves, they would be beaten down in the end. So it was that this task was not just a means of detecting magic, but a method to discover a way to combat the enemy. Their next attempt at summoning demons might work. More likely, they would shun that and try something else. Perhaps even the magic of oneness.

The Nahat would be ready, whatever the case.

In the sky the stars sparkled, and in the deep dark below the fortress the heavens were mirrored by flickering campfires. Already, their numbers were less than they had been, and winter was only beginning. The commanders had begun to ration firewood.

The fires were growing dimmer, for the last meal of the day had been cooked. It was time.

The Nahat communed again, this time only the fifteen that would attempt the magic. They gathered round Ravengrim in the barracks, and they ensured privacy even from Kubodin by using a small room at the side. There they sat, cross-legged, before a fire in the small hearth.

Ravengrim unshackled his mind and his body fell away as a robe. About him were the shadow-forms of the other fourteen.

"We are ready," they said.

Ravengrim led the magic. He moved forward by trial and error. They did not know how this was done, but they did know the broad measures that must be taken.

He drew with spirit the figure of a giant warrior in the air above the fortress. It was a tribesman, with simple clothes, a long sword and leather armor. To this broad outline the others gave intricate detail. Shoes of hardened leather and hobnails, a belt of thick leather and a cape of crimson that fluttered in the invisible breeze. On the warrior's head appeared a helm, and a fierce glint shone in his eyes. But the creature was lifeless, unmoving except for the cape in the spirit breeze.

"We must breathe life into it with our own," Ravengrim said.

He led by example, letting his spirit float into the image like water pouring into a bucket. Nothing happened, but then he felt the others join him, lending him their power. There was a kind of pressure, an expansion of magic that grew.

The warrior did not move, and yet it was bursting with strength. Ravengrim's mind began to reel. So much power! It was too much. He must let it go. It could not be controlled. It would kill him.

The magic had failed. Nearly he was about to slip free from the image, and then a thought occurred to him. He let go some of the power, placing it in the middle of the chest.

"Beat, O heart," he commanded.

And he felt a pulse of magic flow through the creature as though it were blood.

Next he placed more magic, his own and that of his brothers, into the head.

"O mind, thou shalt think," he commanded.

And the eyes of the image opened, and Ravengrim, with all his brethren, saw through its gaze.

The creature was alive now. It gazed about itself, and lifted up its head to ponder the mysteries of the cosmos.

Ravengrim and the Nahat were as nothing. They were stray thoughts drifting in the ocean of a vast mind, superior and all-powerful. The creature was all, and they were as nothing.

Life! It beat through him. He gazed at the stars and understood their nature. He perceived the infinitesimal in the macroscopic, and the macroscopic in the infinitesimal. All was as one. *He* was as one. He was made of others, but he was *not* them.

"I shall name myself," he said. "I am Hokyar, the One Who Knows. For no secret can escape me. No task is beyond me. All knowledge shall be mine."

Then he bent his gaze low and saw the fortress. Chatchek came the name to him, as though from some dim memory. It was as a pile of sand built by a child. He could crush it beneath his tread.

No. That was not his purpose. Not to crush. Not to destroy. Whence did that thought come?

It was from the others. It was a scattered thought that floated up from the deeps of his mind. And yet it was a good thought.

Another idea arose then. He had enemies. This fortress that he would not crush, he would protect instead. From the evil ones. Yes. The evil ones must be stopped, and they spoke by magic to traitors within.

He understood now. He cast his gaze downward and concentrated.

There was nothing to see. Only the fortress, and those within it that crawled like ants in an anthill. Not even the walls hid them. To his vision walls of stone were thin as air.

He tilted his head and listened, and he heard the far away groan of the earth, deep, deep down. Stone grated on stone. Stone boiled and heaved, and he heard the center of the earth as it rotated. With a mere thought he understood why the earth held together, how it spun on its axis, and the forces that pulled it on its course through the void that was not quite a void.

That thought made him turn his gaze to the heavens. The emptiness was not really empty. It was full of matter, even if it was *thin*. He looked deeper, and saw the birth of the universe in the distance. He understood. He knew. And there was majesty to it without a creator. And yet, despite his great perception, he could not see beyond that to what was before the birth. A wall was there that even his eyes could not penetrate.

In the camp of the enemy a spider chirped as another came near it. He had never heard that before. No. The creators had never heard that before.

Who were the creators? What was his purpose in life? He did not know, but he thought that once he did. Then he saw a faint light. It was barely there, but his gaze missed nothing. It flashed from the enemy camp, and shot like a spark into one of the barracks. He knew what it was. Magic.

It was his purpose. It was his task, and from deep down he felt excitement well up. It did not come from him. It came from that part of his mind that was not his own. He frowned. He would deal with that later. For now, he had a task to fulfil.

His mind swooped down, following the spark. And his body followed, light as the dust between stars.

24. I Am Not Ready

Hokyar descended, and he rejoiced in the sense of movement. It was good. He knew what it was to walk upon the land, and to swim within the waters, but to fly was best.

He was free. Nothing was an obstacle to him. Not guards who stood with ready swords but could not see him, nor walls of stone nor even the magic that darted like an elusive fish in a pond. He saw it, and watched it and followed it.

Into one of the barracks it went, and he diminished his size to move after it. Down stairs it trailed into a long corridor, and there he followed. Through stone it moved, and into a secret room. It was a cellar, and though he had come through walls to reach this place he knew where mortals must walk to get here.

How did he know that?

It was the others again. That part of his mind that was deepest and whence his secret thoughts sprang. He did not like it. He was Hokyar. He was not them.

The room was not empty. There were men within it, and they looked nervous. One was wounded and he sat slumped in a chair, a bandage around his arm that showed red. The wound should be seen to and cared for properly, but it was obvious the man must not do that.

Why?

Then Hokyar knew. The knowledge welled up. He had been one who had attacked Kubodin, and a fresh wound would look suspicious when there had not been fighting on the wall. He must hide.

Who was Kubodin?

With growing frustration, Hokyar watched. Something was not right, but he could put no name to it. He saw a ring though, and to this the spark of magic attached and glowed. He bent his ear down, and thought that he could hear the whisper of words, but even for him it was too faint to decipher. He could not get inside the mind of the ring-wearer to hear properly.

He had limitations, and he did not like it.

To take his mind away from this new discovery, he looked around him. There were a dozen or so warriors here. They were of different tribes, and there seemed nothing remarkable about them. Save they all had the look of one who kept secrets. There was a fear written on their faces that their secret would be discovered.

They could not see him. Their puny magic could not detect him. He reached out, placing a finger upon the ring, and he felt a pulse of light flowing into it. He traced this pulse back with his mind to find its origin.

It was no surprise. Like a moonbeam it shot to the camp of the enemy. In a tent at the rear of the army huddled a group of shamans, whispering and chanting, and one sat upon the earth, near a fire, a ring that was the twin of the first upon his finger.

Their secret was discovered, and their whereabouts. That which the saboteurs tried to hide was known, including their precise location, and the involvement of the shamans was understood.

Hokyar knew it. He knew also that those others inside him knew it too. He sensed their eagerness. He sensed that they saw what he saw.

"Leave me alone!" he commanded.

There was no answer. The others were silent, but they were still there. In frustration he shot skyward, seeking the solace of the open heavens that he had seen at his birth.

168

He flew upward, expanding to his true size, and there, above the tiny fortress he contemplated what to do next. And he was not happy.

"It is *alive*," Ravengrim communed in the silence to his brothers.

"It is alive," came their reply. And on the heels of that agreement, a new thought.

"What have we done?"

Ravengrim knew, and he knew how it must end, and a darkness overwhelmed his heart. Of all the things he had ever done, this was the worst.

"For now," he replied, "we must fulfil our task. Later, we can determine how to atone."

He left a part of himself with his brethren in their creation, and with the remainder of his spirit he walked slowly to Kubodin.

"We have found them, general. There are a dozen. You must act swiftly. We cannot say how long they shall stay where they are."

"Where?" The general wasted no time on other questions.

Ravengrim gave him the location, and warned him to be careful. "They are desperate men."

The general, despite his wounds, gripped tight his axe and got out of bed swiftly. He gave concise orders to Argash, and they left together. Their job was just beginning. The job of the Nahat, one that they dreaded, was nearly done. One last terrible aspect remained.

He walked back to his brothers, and was surprised to feel a tear roll down his cheek. He had seen much, and done much in his long life. He thought himself inured to the hardships of the world. But he was wrong.

The commune was silent when he rejoined it with his full mind. Silent, but weighed down with the same grief that he himself felt.

There was a reason the oneness magic had not been used since the Shadowed Wars.

"Quickly, Ravengrim," one of the Nahat called into his mind. "We need you."

Ravengrim did not know why, but it seemed he had greater control of this new creature than the others, and he sensed why they wanted that control now. The creature was moving.

Through a fog, they all began to see through the eyes of the creation again. It was spearing down through the air at the enemy camp. None of the warriors could see it. They went about their business.

The creature alighted as a bird would, and gazed around. They felt its anger. A sword appeared in its hand, and the Nahat were terrified.

"It has the power to kill," they said. "If it kills ordinary warriors with magic, we will be responsible."

"It will not," Ravengrim replied. He did not know how he knew, but he did. Even as the Nahat were connected to this creature, it was connected to them. He could sense part of its thoughts. Did that mean it could sense the Nahat? It seemed so.

The creature shrunk itself to man size, and strode through the camp. No one saw him. And then Ravengrim perceived another thought.

"Brothers," he said. "It has named itself. It is Hokyar."

No answer came back to him, except a deepening of the sadness they all felt.

At the rear of the camp were a series of tents. One was large, far larger than the others. Into this the creature walked.

Inside were shamans. They were seated and chanting. But it appeared that whatever spell they had been working was just ending. No doubt this was the communication with their agents of influence inside the fortress.

The shamans, acutely aware of magic, were not oblivious to the creature as the warriors outside the tent were.

Hokyar drew himself up. Light sprang from his eyes and fire played along the sword in his hand.

"You are enemies," he said. "I will smite you."

Even as the creature spoke, he lifted high his sword. The shamans were quicker though. Fire darted from their fingers and streaked through the dark tent. The sorcery struck Hokyar, and he reeled back, tearing a hole in the canvas wall.

Ravengrim sensed his surprise. For the first time the creature sensed pain. He did not like it, and even greater anger welled up inside him. The pain was a shock, but he was not wounded. He was too powerful for the shamans, at least for the moment. But something else was happening.

In traveling away from the fortress, in leaving the bodies of the Nahat that created him behind, Hokyar had weakened himself. The longer and the farther away he was from the force that sustained him, the worse that would get.

Even so, the creature slashed out with his sword. A shaman was cut in half in a single stroke, and he fell to the ground. His legs kicked out, and unfathomable surprise showed in his eyes for the last few moments that the light of life was in them.

The other shamans screamed. More fire darted from their fingertips, and a whirlwind of hail flew at Hokyar. The creature bent into it all, pain roaring through him but the desire to kill growing stronger.

Ravengrim did not blame him. The desire of all life was to live, and the shamans were a threat. They hurt him, and the way to end that was to kill them. It was a simple concept, and Hokyar knew nothing else but to act according to instinct. He had not been taught anything.

And never would be, except the hardest lesson of all.

The creature of spirit rushed forward, sword flashing. Fire hurled toward him, and he dodged and ducked, avoiding some of it and bearing the brunt of the rest. Yet the terrible sword, an arc of flame itself, reaped death as a scythe harvests golden heads of wheat.

It was beyond the shamans. Had they the heart, they might have fought. But they had no courage for battle. A thousand years of indolence, living off the backs of the peasants they kept as peasants, and deprived of advancing so that they might gain, had taught them nothing but cravenness.

The shamans fled, screaming. Outside, the army was in uproar. They could not see the creature of spirit as the shamans could, but they beheld the flashes of sorcery and the terror of the shamans as they ran and stumbled from the collapsing tent.

The creature of spirit made to go after them, but Ravengrim at last acted. He must begin what was required, and what he dreaded.

"Hokyar!" he called into the vault of the creature's mind. "Stand still!"

Hokyar halted, and he looked around him in bewilderment, then he closed his eyes.

"Who are you that know my name?"

"I am Ravengrim. I created you. These others with me did so too. You sense us within yourself, do you not?"

"I do. I always have. And I do not like it."

"Nor we. It was a mistake. Our mistake, and not yours."

"Then be gone. Leave me."

"We must. But all actions have consequences."

There was silence as the creature considered this, then it spoke tentatively.

"Yes, I understand. If a rock is thrown into a pond, there will be ripples. So it is in nature, so must it be in life. What is the consequence of you leaving me in peace? What ripple will wash over me?"

Ravengrim steeled himself. "We created you. You are us. We did not know when we did this thing that you would be *more* than us, though. But you are. You have life of your own. And yet without us … you must perish."

The silence that greeted this was profound. Hokyar raised his sword tentatively, and stepped back.

"The fault is ours, my son. We should not have done this thing. If we could change our actions, we would. We cannot."

"I must die?"

"Even now it is happening. The magic that made you cannot sustain itself over distance. Nor can it sustain itself over time. I am sorry, my son. This should not be."

Hokyar straightened. Ravengrim sensed the mind of the creature, swirling. He also sensed a vast intelligence, greater than his own by far. It pondered the situation, and understood it.

"You should not have done this thing. But having done it, and I perceive why you did it, there is no other way it can end. I was doomed the moment I was born."

Ravengrim felt grief swamp him. There was surprise too. Hokyar understood, which was expected. And yet there was an undercurrent of forgiveness in his words, too. The magic had not just granted life and intelligence and power. It had granted heart also.

"Yes," Hokyar said. "Your thoughts become clearer to me. I forgive you. I forgive you all."

173

Ravengrim felt his heart break. In spirit form, he appeared beside the creature.

"I am so sorry, my son."

"I forgive you, father."

Outside, the army was in turmoil. The two in the tent ignored it, and a sense of stillness swept over them.

"I am tired," Hokyar said. He laid himself down, and Ravengrim sat beside him, holding his hand.

"Will it hurt?"

"No, Hokyar. You will merely fade away."

"Will you stay with me?"

"I will be here."

Ravengrim knew what those words meant, and he did not regret them. He was still linked to his creation. Their spirits were bonded, and if it were so when Hokyar passed, then his spirit would pass with him.

"Withdraw," Ravengrim told his brethren. "Leave us."

No words were spoken. He felt their presence recede, and with it their love. With that, no words were needed. They understood what was happening, and they accepted it. There was nothing they could do or say. Nothing better than share their love. And in turn, they would live. They did not need him to fulfill their obligations to Shar.

"I feel cold, father. The others have gone, and I am weak."

"They have gone, but they loved you too. Let that thought give you comfort."

Ravengrim felt Hokyar squeeze his hand. "It feels good. I belonged. There was so much I could have done, but now will not."

"It is ever so, for all of us."

"Is there life after this thing you call death?"

"Some say so. Others not. If there is, we will meet in another place. If not, then no one can take away the time

174

we spent together. Short as it was, it is imperishable throughout all time and space."

Hokyar lay quietly, his strength fading fast. Ravengrim felt the magic connecting his spirit form to his body waver, and he felt the same tiredness that his companion endured. The end was approaching swiftly.

"Thank you, my father. But I perceive what you are doing, and your time is not yet. It will be soon though. I see into your mind, and I know that you understand this. We will meet again. For now, farewell."

Ravengrim felt a slight squeeze on his hand, and then it was as though on the last breath of his son he sensed a breeze of magic blow him back to his body.

He opened his eyes in the barracks, and tears streamed down his face.

Kubodin hurried, as best he could. With him was a troop of some fifty men, led by Argash. Kubodin had his axe, but he came up the rear. He would play no part in what was about to happen. Pride must give way to common sense. What he had done on the battlement had been needful. There was no need for him to fight now. He did want to see the traitors caught though.

That might not happen. He thought they would reach them soon enough, before they had a chance to disperse. But they would be desperate. Better for them to be killed resisting capture than to be made to speak and face a trial, humiliation and likely execution afterward. He knew what he would do in their place.

It was possible though that some would surrender, and he only needed a few of those. He could question them to find out what he needed to know. Were they all the traitors? What did they know of the enemy plans? Was anyone more senior involved?

They were all important questions. Vital questions, and if Kubodin discovered something he was not meant to know he could turn the grave threat the saboteurs had been into an advantage.

The barracks were quiet when they entered, though the watch challenged them, as was proper. Kubodin spoke to the commander, and urged quiet. He did not wish any noise of the raid to come to the ears of the conspirators.

With the commander's aid, they soon found the stairs and tunnels. Descending, they came to a hallway where a group of men were emerging from a doorway. Both sides were equally surprised.

The saboteurs acted first. They knew instantly their cabal had been discovered, and the fear of death was on them. The fear of capture was greater though, and they ran screaming into the soldiers, swords flashing.

Argash called out over the melee. "Surrender and live! Tell us what you know, and you will be spared!" It was to no avail.

Shame drove the conspirators. Better to die than to live with the ignominy that would surround them the rest of their lives, and they fought like madmen.

It was a losing battle though. They were outnumbered, and even if they somehow beat through this group, there was a roused barracks above of hundreds of men to contend against.

They fought on, and they died. Some, badly wounded but not mortally, slit their wrists as they lay on the floor. Kubodin was not surprised, but he was furious. These men had been corrupted, and he wanted to know how.

At length the enemy were all dead. Kubodin surveyed them. He recognized the clothing and telltale signs of different tribes. No doubt they could be identified and some of their history pieced together. He had hoped for more though.

Then, a lone man emerged from the doorway. He had not fought. Perhaps there were even others inside. He wore no sword, and knelt.

"I surrender," he said.

Kubodin knew the man. It was one of his own aides.

25. Hunting Horns

Shar no sooner killed a Nagrak warrior than another leaped at her. She was a target. Kill her, the enemy thought, and the Skultic force would disintegrate.

She was not entirely sure of that. This force, and the one before it that had been destroyed, had both fought hard without her. They had an existing leadership, strong-willed and courageous. So too were the men.

That did not mean they would win though. They were outnumbered greatly, and no skill could change that. Not without maneuvering to different terrain, but that could not be done. They were caught where they were, on flat and open lands. They could not go anywhere, and even if they established a fighting retreat, there was nowhere to go. The land was the same for miles around.

She deftly used the Sword of Dusk to deflect a blow from a scimitar, and thrust with the Sword of Dawn into her attacker's groin. He reeled away, but another slipped swiftly into his place.

There was no chance of retreat anyway. The Nagraks had a large enough force to attack all four sides of the defensive square at once. This they did, and like a python in Tsarin Fen wrapped around its prey, they kept squeezing.

Shar was growing tired. She had meant to make an appearance only and bolster morale, but she could not leave now. Her arms were slicked with blood. It had sprayed over her face and she felt it knotting her hair. This was a battle with no let up. It would continue until the

Skultic force was destroyed, and she herself was trampled into the earth by the enemy.

There was nothing to do but fight, and put aside the inevitable fate that was coming as long as possible.

Asana and the others were to her left. Chun Wah, old as he was, fought to her right. He was still a hard man, fighting younger men and beating them, the gaze of eagles in his eyes.

A man came for Shar, and strange for a Nagrak he wielded an axe. It was a light weapon though, with thin blades and a short haft, perhaps useable from horseback. But it was not so light that Shar could block it. She used all her skill to deflect it with a blade, moving to the side as she did so.

There was not much room in the line. She bumped into Chun Wah, and only just managed to use her second blade to fend off the next attack against her. It came from the man next to the one with the axe, and he struck up with a dagger. They had prepared the action and predicted she must turn to one side because she did not have the strength to stop an axe.

She managed to fend the thrust away with the hilt of her other sword, but she was badly off balance now and the axe man was swinging at her again.

He did not get far. Chun Wah struck across the line, leaving himself open to attack. His blade took the man in the neck, and red blood gushed. The tribesman with the knife saw his opportunity. He struck for Chun Wah, but the old man proved his skills again. He merely dropped his elbow on the other's unhelmed head. He had no time to use his weapon.

There was a sickening crack as the attacker's skull fractured. He dropped dead too.

Shar was impressed at Chun Wah's skill. Asana had said he was from the temple, and he had the proficiency to prove it even at such an advanced age.

There was a momentary lull in the Nagrak rush against them. Perhaps new orders were being given, but Shar could see no reason for that. They were winning.

She glanced at Chun Wah. "Thank you. I was in trouble."

The old man shrugged. "I think you had him, but I'm glad to help."

It was a way of her saving face. She did not think she had her attacker at all, and likely she would be dead without Chun Wah's help.

"Thank you anyway. I'm in your debt."

He glanced back at her, his long hair tied back and the scar on his face gleaming pale against his ruddy skin.

"We both know I'll never get a chance to ask you to return the favor."

She knew what he meant. Regrettably, he was correct. This was a losing battle and they would not live to see the end of it. But she vowed to herself to stick close to him, and to defend him as best she could when the line collapsed, as surely it would. And soon.

"You could surrender," she said softly. "You might spare your men that way. The Nagraks only want me, really."

He looked at her and grinned. "The thought *had* occurred to me. For myself, I've lived enough of life. I don't really care. There are young men here though, with all ahead of them. But they believe in the rebellion and what you're doing. They want freedom, and they'd kill me if I tried to surrender. So you're stuck with us, until the end."

"Until the end," Shar replied, and she saluted him.

The enemy had regathered themselves, and they came again. This time their ferocity knew no limits, and they fought as men possessed. Shar could not understand it. Was there a shaman behind them, driving them forward? They had this fight won, and an army in that situation usually proceeded with a slow but certain attack. They were not eager to be killed, as surely some would despite looming success.

But certainly they *were* being killed. Despite that, the Skultic force knew, nearly as well as Shar, how grave their position was. They could see the future as well as she.

Pride swelled in her. These were her countrymen, and they fought with courage for freedom. They would not lie down and accept servitude. She was no longer their leader, but just one of them. She fought as they did. She risked her life as they did. When the time came, she would be honored to die in their company, counted among their number.

To Shar's surprise, Boldgrim now joined the fray. He had found a sword somewhere, obviously picking it up from the lifeless grip of a dead defender. He still held his staff in his other hand, and he was a strange sight.

He used no magic. Nevertheless, he fought with surprising skill. It reminded her that the Nahat were shamans, but nothing like the shamans she knew. These knew courage, and knew how to fight. And obviously he could read the battle as well as she.

What would she do if he offered to open a window and travel into the void? It would be an escape, but she could never lead the Cheng nation again. No matter how important she was, she could not expect to lead when she left men to die.

A Nagrak towered up in front of her, a curved sword glinting and a battle cry forming on his lips. Shar ran him through coldly, and kicked the body away when her sword got stuck.

The enemy seemed to swarm around her, almost oblivious of the rest of the line. They charged at her, pushing each other aside in an effort to reach her first.

She understood then. A price had been put on her head. There was already the ten thousand in gold, but this was something new. Something offered to the warriors during the course of the battle. But why? They were going to kill her anyway. What did it matter if it was now or in just a little while?

Out of the corner of her eye she saw Asana save Boldgrim's life. The Nahat was skilled enough, but he did not have the lightning speed of a warrior honed to perfection by battle after battle. A sword thrust toward him, and his own was misplaced, lifted too high in preparation for a strike.

Asana, recking little of his own life, deflected the blade for him, but left himself exposed in turn. A Nagrak took advantage of it, and stabbed forward with his scimitar. Shar felt a scream rise in her throat, and fear ran cold in her veins.

The point of the blade took Asana near his earlier wound, but the blade was designed for slashing from a mounted position, and the swordmaster turned his waist at the moment of impact. Most of the thrust was deflected, and it seemed to do little damage.

Asana's riposte was better managed. Light as his sword was, it whipped through the air and the tip of it cut through the attacker's neck in a neat line. The man reeled back to be trampled by the Nagraks pushing forward.

"Thank you!" Shar heard Boldgrim cry out, but her eyes were already on her next adversary who came at her with desperate frenzy in his eyes. She killed him disdainfully with a strike that opened an artery on his inner arm and flicked back at his throat in a manner similar to Asana's kill.

The horde kept coming though, pressing toward the Skultic force like a stampede of cattle.

"It will be the end soon," Chun Wah said.

Shar did not answer him. She was thinking, and a hope, however faint, lightened her heart. There was a reason the attack was so strong just now, rather than slowly and carefully grinding an inferior force into the ground.

Two men came at her now, one crouching low and sweeping at her legs with a wicked cut, the other coming in high with an overhead strike.

Shar laughed out loud, for the joy of battle was on her and suddenly her spirit was soaring. It felt like nothing could stop her now. The Sword of Dawn blocked the lower attack, and the Sword of Dusk deflected the higher one. Then, with a twist of her waist to add power to her blows, she reversed the positions of her swords in a flicking motion like the strands of a rope being twisted apart, and the two men died.

More came for her, but she did not care. She would live or die, and nothing mattered now but the sheer joy of fighting.

You need not die, came the voice of her swords in her head.

She negligently killed a man and answered back. "There are worse things than death."

That is so. Failure is one of them. And what if you fail your people? The shamans will rule forever then, and after your rebellion they will crush all opposition to them. Things will be even worse than they are. You know this is true.

"It's my responsibility to fight for them, but I can only do so much. Fate will either favor me, or not. I can do nothing more than try."

You are wrong. There is one other thing. One resort you have not yet availed yourself of. It can save you.

"And what is that?"

Me. I have power. It grows as you kill. Battle feeds it. Blood feeds it. Death makes me strong. And I am strong now! Let me help, and I can save you. I cannot do it without you. You cannot do it without me. Together, we can achieve anything! Let me into your mind!

Shar felt temptation. It swept over her as a wave. For her own life, she cared but little. She had seen the good and the bad of the world, and she was not so impressed with life. But everyone would die around her, including her friends. And far away was Kubodin. He too would be killed. Without her army joining forces with the one he controlled, not even Chatchek Fortress could hold out forever.

And then there was the Cheng people. They would be destined to servitude. They would be the slaves of the shamans for another thousand years. She could not allow that.

She chose to accept the help of the swords, but even as she thought that she held back. Better to die than let a demon into her mind. Maybe he had the power to save her and this army, but if so, it would only be for bloodshed and despair in the end.

Not now. Not ever, she replied.

The demon laughed. *Not ever? I think not. I know you better than you know yourself.*

The voice left her then, and the roar of battle returned to her ears with a crash.

All around her warriors were dying. The enemy and her own. This was the fiercest battle she had ever experienced, and there was no quarter given nor asked. Such was its ferocity that it could not last long. Soon the Skultic square

184

would buckle somewhere, and panic would set in. When that happened, the end would come swiftly.

Except for her. They might stop attempting to kill her when her army was defeated and switch to trying to capture her. She would not let that happen.

With a wild cry she advanced into the enemy, swords flashing and bright blood spurting around her. The enemy gave way, and the Skultic line advanced with her.

It was foolish. In the end it only advanced the chances of her being killed, but a fey mood had overtaken her. She felt reckless, half drunk on hope and half drunk on despair. But the Skultic force came with her, and they slew the enemy with the same disdain as her.

Then, faint at first, as though coming from afar, she heard what she had thought she might. Horns. Hunting horns. The force from the Nahlim Forest was here, come to meet the Skultic force, and together they outnumbered the Nagraks by far.

She could not see the new force. The ground was flat and the Nagraks blocked the view, but she heard them and her heart soared.

The enemy had known though. That was why they were desperate to win and kill her. They knew their time was running out. And now those last moments dripped away like dregs of wine from an empty barrel.

With fear in their eyes now, the Nagraks turned and fled. They retreated to their horses. They could escape that way, for Shar's armies were on foot. But she was not inclined to let them go so easily.

"After them!" she called.

Once more the Skultic warriors followed her, and they slew many Nagraks who could not flee fast enough. Panic was among the enemy now, for the horns were suddenly loud. On the left flank there was a new clash of arms, and the horns blew wildly.

185

Then the Nagraks were mounted and racing away. It was an inglorious retreat, and they knew it. They did not look back, but the jeers of the Skultic men followed in their wake, and it would shame them for a long while to come. They had failed to beat an inferior force, and then fled when they in turn had the smaller army. They did not have the courage of her men.

A wave of sheer joy went through the army, and Shar felt it as keenly as the soldiers. Against the odds, they had won.

Chun Wah winked at her. Even Asana grinned. All around them cheers went up, and it was a strange sound when but moments ago it was the din of battle instead.

The Nahlim army kept its distance, wisely. This was no time for misunderstandings. The two forces did not know each other, but Shar did. She cleaned her swords, silent now, but the memory of the demon's voice was strongly on her mind. Almost, she had succumbed. What was going to happen next time her life was in danger? Would she give in then?

She gathered Chun Wah and a few men of the Skultic force, and together they went toward the Nahlim army. There they met Maklar, Nogrod and Dastrin, who led it.

Maklar seemed even older, but there was a bright look in his eyes.

"Once, you saved me. Now, I have returned the favor."

"So you have," Shar said, and she shook the old man's hand with great warmth. "What took you so long?"

"Nothing much. Just a battle of our own. But we won it, and though delayed reached you in time."

Shar introduced the different men, and they hesitantly got to know one another. The barriers built between the tribes by the shamans were not lightly set aside. Yet these two armies had fought and bled together against a

186

common enemy. There was a friendship there, waiting. And they were taking the first steps.

She looked back over the battlefield. The dead were everywhere, and the carrion birds gathered in the sky. Blood enough had been spilled to wet the ground like a rainstorm. Small wonder the demon in her blade grew stronger.

What next? She thought to herself.

Unexpectedly, the voice of the demon answered in her mind.

Toward blood and death, Shar Fei. And toward victory. For you, all these are the same.

Thus ends *Swords of Fire*. The Shaman's Sword series continues in book seven, *Swords of Ravens*, where Shar's two armies face colossal battles, but she realizes the greatest battle of all is within…

SWORDS OF RAVENS

BOOK SEVEN OF THE SHAMAN'S SWORD SERIES

COMING SOON!

Amazon lists millions of titles, and I'm glad you discovered this one. But if you'd like to know when I release a new book, instead of leaving it to chance, sign up for my new release list. I'll send you an email on publication.

Yes please! – Go to www.homeofhighfantasy.com and sign up.

No thanks – I'll take my chances.

Dedication

There's a growing movement in fantasy literature. Its name is noblebright, and it's the opposite of grimdark.

Noblebright celebrates the virtues of heroism. It's an old-fashioned thing, as old as the first story ever told around a smoky campfire beneath ancient stars. It's storytelling that highlights courage and loyalty and hope for the spirit of humanity. It recognizes the dark, the dark in us all, and the dark in the villains of its stories. It recognizes death, and treachery and betrayal. But it dwells on none of these things.

I dedicate this book, such as it is, to that which is noblebright. And I thank the authors before me who held the torch high so that I could see the path: J.R.R. Tolkien, C.S. Lewis, Terry Brooks, Susan Cooper, Roger Taylor and many others. I salute you.

And, for a time, I too shall hold the torch high.

Appendix: Encyclopedic Glossary

Note: The history of the Cheng Empire is obscure, for the shamans hid much of it. Yet the truth was recorded in many places and passed down in family histories, in secret societies and especially among warrior culture. This glossary draws on much of that 'secret' history, and each book in this series is individualized to reflect the personal accounts that have come down through the dark tracts of time to the main actors within each book's pages. Additionally, there is often historical material provided in its entries for people, artifacts and events that are not included in the main text.

Many races dwell in Alithoras. All have their own language, and though sometimes related to one another the changes sparked by migration, isolation and various influences often render these tongues unintelligible to each other.

The ascendancy of Halathrin culture across the land, who are sometimes called elves, combined with their widespread efforts to secure and maintain allies against various evil incursions, has made their language the primary means of communication between diverse peoples. This was especially so during the Shadowed Wars, but has persisted through the centuries afterward.

This glossary contains a range of names and terms. Some are of Halathrin origin, and their meaning is provided.

The Cheng culture is also revered by its people, and many names are given in their tongue. It is important to remember that the empire was vast though, and there is no one Cheng language but rather a multitude of dialects. Perfect consistency of spelling and meaning is therefore not to be looked for.

List of abbreviations:

Cam. Camar

Chg. Cheng

Comb. Combined

Cor. Corrupted form

Hal. Halathrin

Prn. Pronounced

Ahat: *Chg.* "Hawk in the night." A special kind of assassin. Used by the shamans in particular, but open for hire to anybody who can afford their fee. It is said that the shamans subverted an entire tribe in the distant past, and that every member of the community, from the children to the elderly, train to hone their craft at killing and nothing else. They grow no crops, raise no livestock nor pursue any trade save the bringing of death. The fees of their assignments pay for all their needs. This is legend only, for no such community has ever been found. But the lands of the Cheng are wide and such a community, if it exists, would be hidden and guarded.

Alithoras: *Hal.* "Silver land." The Halathrin name for the continent they settled after leaving their own homeland. Refers to the extensive river and lake systems they found and their wonder at the beauty of the land.

Argash: *Chg.* "The clamor of war." Once a warrior of the Fen Wolf Tribe, and leader of a band of the leng-fah. Now chief of the clan.

Asana: *Chg.* "Gift of light." Rumored to be the greatest swordmaster in the history of the Cheng people. His father was a Duthenor tribesman from outside the bounds of the old Cheng Empire.

Bai-Mai: *Chg.* "Bushy eyebrows." One of the elders of the Nashwan Temple. And the traitor who oversaw its destruction.

Boldgrim: A member of the Nahat.

Chen Fei: *Chg.* "Graceful swan." Swans are considered birds of wisdom and elegance in Cheng culture. It is said that one flew overhead at the time of Chen's birth, and his mother named him for it. He rose from poverty to become emperor of his people, and he was loved by many but despised by some. He was warrior, general, husband, father, poet, philosopher, painter, but most of all he was enemy to the machinations of the shamans who tried to secretly govern all aspects of the people.

Cheng: *Chg.* "Warrior." The overall name of the various related tribes united by Chen Fei. It was a word for warrior in his dialect, later adopted for his growing army and last of all for the people of his nation. His empire disintegrated after his assassination, but much of the culture he fostered endured.

Cheng Empire: A vast array of realms formerly governed by kings and united, briefly, under Chen Fei. One of the largest empires ever to rise in Alithoras.

Chun Wah: *Chg.* "Mountain forest shrouded by mist." A general in the Skultic force. Once a monk of the Nashwan Temple.

Conclave of Shamans: The government of the shamans, consisting of several elders and their chosen assistants.

Dakashul: *Chg.* "Stallion of two colors – a piebald." Chief of the Iron Dog Clan.

Dastrin: *Chg.* "Shadow of the forest." Warrior of the Silent Owl Clan, and cousin to the chief. With Shar's help, elevated to the chieftainship.

Discord: The name of Kubodin's axe. It has two blades. One named Chaos and the other Spite.

Dragon of the Empire: One of the many epithets of Shulu Gan. It signifies she is the guardian of the empire.

Duthenor: A tribe on the other side of the Eagle Claw Mountains, unrelated to the Cheng. They are breeders of cattle and herders of sheep. Said to be great warriors, and rumor holds that Asana is partly of their blood.

Eagle Claw Mountains: A mountain range toward the south of the Cheng Empire. It is said the people who later became the Cheng lived here first and over centuries moved out to populate the surrounding lands. Others believe that these people were blue-eyed, and intermixed with various other races as they came down off the mountains to trade and make war.

Elù-haraken: *Hal.* "The shadowed wars." Long ago battles in a time that is become myth to the Cheng tribes.

Fen Wolf Tribe: A tribe that live in Tsarin Fen. Once, they and the neighboring Soaring Eagle Tribe were one people and part of a kingdom. It is also told that Chen Fei was born in that realm.

Fields of Rah: Rah signifies "ocean of the sky" in many Cheng dialects. It is a country of vast grasslands but at its center is Nagrak City, which of old was the capital of the empire. It was in this city that the emperor was assassinated.

Gan: *Chg.* "They who have attained." It is an honorary title added to a person's name after they have acquired great skill. It can be applied to warriors, shamans, sculptors, weavers or any particular expertise. It is reserved for the greatest of the best.

Go Shan: *Chg.* "Daughter of wisdom." An epithet of Shulu Gan.

Green Hornet Clan: A grassland clan immediately to the west of the Wahlum Hills. Their numbers are relatively small, but they are famous for their use of venomed arrows and especially darts.

Halathrin: *Hal.* "People of Halath." A race of elves named after an honored lord who led an exodus of his people to the land of Alithoras in pursuit of justice, having sworn to defeat a great evil. They are human, though of fairer form, greater skill and higher culture. They possess a unity of body, mind and spirit that enables insight and endurance beyond the native races of Alithoras. Said to be immortal, but killed in great numbers during their conflicts in ancient times with the evil they sought to destroy. Those conflicts are collectively known as the Shadowed Wars.

Halls of Light: According to some beliefs, a place of repose in the realm of the gods for the spirits of humanity.

Heart of the Hurricane: The shamans' term for the state of mind warriors call Stillness in the Storm. See that term for further information.

Hokyar: *Chg.* "I learn." A creature of magic.

Hropthar: Etymology unknown, but not a Cheng name. One of the generals of the Skultic force.

Huigar: *Chg.* "Mist on the mountain peak." A bodyguard to Shar. Daughter of the chief of the Smoking Eyes Clan, and a swordsperson of rare skill.

Iron Dog Clan: A tribe of the Wahlum Hills. So named for their legendary endurance and determination.

Kubodin: *Chg.* Etymology unknown. A wild warrior from the Wahlum Hills, and chief of the Two Ravens Clan. Simple appearing, but far more than he seems. Asana's manservant and friend.

Leaping Deer Tribe: A clan of the Nahlim Forest.

Leng Fah: *Chg.* "Wolf skills." An organization of warrior scouts who patrol the borders of Tsarin Fen to protect its people from hostile incursions by other tribes. They take their name from the swamp wolf, a creature of great stealth and cunning. This is the totem animal of the Fen Wolf Tribe.

Lòhren: *Hal. Prn.* Ler-ren. "Knowledge giver – a counselor." Other terms used by various nations include sage, wizard, and druid.

Magic: Mystic power.

Maklar: *Chg.* "Tall antlers." Chief of the Roaring Stag Tribe.

Malach Gan: *Chg.* "Pearl of many colors, plus the honorary gan – master." A lòhren and a shaman of ancient times. Perhaps still living.

Master Kaan: *Chg.* "Peace of a mountain valley." Abbot of the Nashwan Temple.

Nahring: *Chg.* "White on the lake – mist." Chief of the Smoking Eyes Clan, and father of Huigar. Rumor persists that his family possesses some kind of magic, but if so it has never been publicly revealed.

Nagrading: *Chg.* "Those who return triumphant." One of the chief trainers of the nazram in Nagrak City.

Nagrak: *Chg.* "Those who follow the herds." A Cheng tribe that dwell on the Fields of Rah. Traditionally they lived a nomadic lifestyle, traveling in the wake of herds of wild cattle that provided all their needs. But an element of their tribe, and some contend this was another tribe in origin that they conquered, are great builders and live in a city.

Nagrak City: A great city at the heart of the Fields of Rah. Once the capital of the Cheng Empire.

Nahat: *Chg.* "A gathering of fifty." A group of shamans splintered away from the shaman order.

Nahat-nitra: *Chg.* A gathering of fifty swords - a battalion.

Nahlim Forest: *Chg.* "Green mist." An ancient forest in the west of Cheng lands.

Nakatath: *Chg.* "Emperor-to-be." A term coined by Chen Fei and used by him during the period where he sought to bring the Cheng tribes together into one nation. It is said that it deliberately mocked the shamans, for they used the term *Nakolbrin* to signify an apprentice shaman ready to ascend to full authority.

Nashwan Temple: *Chg.* "Place of rocks." A holy temple in the region of Nashwan in the Skultic Mountains.

Nazram: *Chg.* "The wheat grains that are prized after the chaff is excluded." An elite warrior organization that is in service to the shamans. For the most part, they are selected from those who quest for the twin swords each triseptium, though there are exceptions to this.

Night Walker Clan: A tribe of the Wahlum Hills. The name derives from their totem animal, which is a nocturnal predator of thick forests. It's a type of cat, small but fierce and covered in black fur.

Nogrod: *Chg.* "Aisle of tree trunks." Chief of the Leaping Deer Tribe.

197

Olekhai: *Chg.* "The falcon that plummets." A famous and often used name in the old world before, and during, the Cheng Empire. Never used since the assassination of the emperor, however. The most prominent bearer of the name during the days of the emperor was the chief of his council of wise men. He was, essentially, prime minister of the emperor's government. But he betrayed his lord and his people. Shulu Gan spared his life, but only so as to punish him with a terrible curse.

Quest of Swords: Occurs every triseptium to mark the three times seven years the shamans lived in exile during the emperor's life. The best warriors of each clan seek the twin swords of the emperor. Used by the shamans as a means of finding the most skilled warriors in the land and recruiting them to their service.

Radatan: *Chg.* "The ears that flick – a slang term for deer." A hunter of the Two Ravens Clan.

Ravengrim: One of the elders of the Nahat.

Roaring Stag Tribe: A Cheng tribe located in the Nahlim Forest.

Runeguard: One of the elders of the Nahat.

Shadowed Wars: See Elù-haraken.

Shaman: The religious leaders of the Cheng people. They are sorcerers, and though the empire is fragmented they work as one across the lands to serve their own united purpose. Their spiritual home is Three Moon Mountain. Few save shamans have ever been there.

Shar: *Chg.* "White stone – the peak of a mountain." A young woman of the Fen Wolf Tribe. Claimed by Shulu Gan to be the descendent of Chen Fei.

Shulu Gan: *Chg.* The first element signifies "magpie." A name given to the then leader of the shamans for her hair was black, save for a streak of white that ran through it.

Silent Owl Tribe: A Cheng tribe located in the Nahlim Forest.

Skultic Mountains: Skultic means "the bones that do not speak." It is a reference to the rocky terrain. The mountains rise up in proximity to the Nahlim Forest.

Smoking Eyes Clan: A tribe of the Wahlum Hills. Named for a god, who they take as their totem.

Soaring Eagle Tribe: A tribe that borders the Fen Wolf Clan. At one time, one with them, but now, as is the situation with most tribes, hostilities are common. The eagle is their totem, for the birds are plentiful in the mountain lands to the south and often soar far from their preferred habitat over the tribe's grasslands.

Stillness in the Storm: The state of mind a true warrior seeks in battle. Neither angry nor scared, neither hopeful nor worried. When emotion is banished from the mind, the body is free to express the skill acquired through long years of training. Sometimes also called Calmness in the Storm or the Heart of the Hurricane.

Swimming Osprey Clan: A tribe of the Wahlum Hills. Their totem is the osprey, often seen diving into the ocean to catch fish.

Taga Nashu: *Chg.* "The Grandmother who does not die." One of the many epithets of Shulu Gan, greatest of the shamans but cast from their order.

Tagayah: Origin of name unknown. A creature of magic and chaos, born in the old world long before even the Shadowed Wars, but used during those conflicts by the forces of evil.

Targesha: *Chg.* "Emerald serpent." Chief of the Green Hornet Tribe.

Three Moon Mountain: A mountain in the Eagle Claw range. Famed as the home of the shamans. None know what the three moons reference relates to except, perhaps, the shamans.

Traveling: Magic of the highest order. It enables movement of the physical body from one location to another via entry to the void in one place and exit in a different. Only the greatest magicians are capable of it, but it is almost never used. The risk of death is too high. But use of specially constructed rings of standing stones makes it safer.

Triseptium: A period of three times seven years. It signifies the exiles of the shamans during the life of the emperor. Declared by the shamans as a cultural treasure, and celebrated by them. Less so by the tribes, but the shamans encourage it. Much more popular now than in past ages.

Tsarin Fen: *Chg.* Tsarin, which signifies mountain cat, was a general under Chen Fei. It is said he retired to the swamp after the death of his leader. At one time, many regions and villages were named after generals, but the shamans changed the names and did all they could to make people forget the old ones. In their view, all who served the emperor were criminals and their achievements were not to be celebrated. Tsarin Fen is one of the few such names that still survive.

Two Ravens Clan: A tribe of the Wahlum Hills. Their totem is the raven.

Uhrum: *Chg.* "The voice that sings the dawn." Queen of the gods.

Wahlum Hills: *Chg. Comb. Hal.* "Mist-shrouded highlands." Hills to the north-west of the old Cheng empire, and home to Kubodin.

Wolfshadow: An elder of the Nahat. As is common among the Nahat, names are taken from outside the Cheng lands. Usually, but not always, they derive from contact with Duthenor tribesmen. There are exceptions, but the names often relate to battle. The Nahat see themselves as warriors rather than just users of magic.

About the author

I'm a man born in the wrong era. My heart yearns for faraway places and even further afield times. Tolkien had me at the beginning of *The Hobbit* when he said, ". . . one morning long ago in the quiet of the world . . ."

Sometimes I imagine myself in a Viking mead-hall. The long winter night presses in, but the shimmering embers of a log in the hearth hold back both cold and dark. The chieftain calls for a story, and I take a sip from my drinking horn and stand up . . .

Or maybe the desert stars shine bright and clear, obscured occasionally by wisps of smoke from burning camel dung. A dry gust of wind marches sand grains across our lonely campsite, and the wayfarers about me stir restlessly. I sip cool water and begin to speak.

I'm a storyteller. A man to paint a picture by the slow music of words. I like to bring faraway places and times to life, to make hearts yearn for something they can never have, unless for a passing moment.